Guys and Ghosts

Jane Lockyer Willis

TSL Publications

First published in Great Britain in 2018
By TSL Publications, Rickmansworth

Copyright © 2018 Jane Lockyer Willis

ISBN / 978-1-912416-19-6

Cover image credits:
https://pixabay.com/en/ghosts-gespenter-spooky-horror-572038/
https://pixabay.com/en/pig-vietnamese-boar-suid%C3%A9
2528356/
https://pixabay.com/en/ghost-vintage-woman-girl-halloween-
977157/

Dedication

To the memory of my son, James,
who, possessing a great sense of humour and fun,
encouraged me to write this novel.

 one

Freddie Pearson stood in front of the mirror flexing his pecs and biceps. His muscles, recently pumped from weights, were plump, taut and shiny. Turning three quarters on, he bent his left leg, flexed his quads, adopted a deep voice, and raised one eyebrow: 'Hey, Baby!' He sighed, relaxed and stared absently out of the bathroom window. At least he could tell Sophie about his interview when he saw her tonight, whereas he wasn't sure about the other: better not tell her about that – not yet, any rate.

Switching on his electric shaver, he examined his face for stray hairs and spots. When you were in Sophie's presence: speaking to her, gazing into those gorgeous brown eyes, you were sorely tempted to share your confidences. She had that way of looking at you as though you were special. Made you feel safe – so safe in fact you wanted to tell her your deepest, darkest secret. He cringed. She'd probably laugh, think him weird: some kind of crackpot. But if he didn't tell her she might find out, and that would be worse. Freddie guessed there were several of his mates who knew, probably tittered about him behind his back. He didn't fancy being the butt of some bloke's joke, not when she was around. Now hang on! What had he to be ashamed of? Just because he was different – no crime in that. Not long now and he'd have enough material to write a book and what was more, it would be based on personal, first hand experience.

He ran a comb through his straight blond hair, drew in his already flat tummy and pulled on his running shorts. Right! She should know. It was his duty to tell her. Relationships were supposed to be based on trust, weren't they? If he loved Sophie – really loved her, then he must learn to trust her and importantly, she must learn to trust him.

'Freddie!' his mother called from downstairs. 'You coming to church?'

He cringed. Church? Why would he want to go to church? 'No, mum.'

'It's the curate's first Sunday.'

'You go. I've got things to do.'

Marching to the bathroom window, he threw it open; took large lungfuls of sharp, autumnal air and then shut it with a resounding bang.

Right! He'd decided. He would tell her tonight, at the Pizza Parlour.

Ø Ø

George Theodore Pym looked plaintively at his wife. 'You moved into the spare room again last night.'

'I'm sorry, but I can't stand it – I really can't.' Her voice was tight, strained. 'I must get my sleep; you know that.'

There followed an uncomfortable silence, during which George adjusted his clerical collar and straightened his stock before going in search of an extra jersey to put on under his cassock.

He always knew when he had been snoring – his mouth felt dry and his throat sore. But how to stop! He had tried everything: rings in his nose, acupuncture, alarms – the lot. Nothing worked. When he and Sheila slept together, she was irritable and exhausted the next day – clear confirmation that he'd kept her awake. Now little vexations and resentments lay agitating between them. Recently George had begun to feel a cold spot in the pit of his stomach. He supposed it might be fear, fear that she no longer loved him. He shivered. Even with his extra jersey, George felt chilled to the core. How much longer did they have to wait before the church commissioners sorted out the new rectory?

'I'm off then.' He picked up his *Book of Common Prayer*

from the hall table, kissed her briefly on the cheek and walked to the front door. 'You *are* coming to church?' He was never quite sure how the mood would take her and frequently looked up from his prayer desk to find her absent from the front pew.

'Of course I'm coming to church, George,' she said, handing him the small, leather case that held his surplice and stole. 'I'm as curious as anyone to see our new curate.'

Ø Ø

At eight thirty, Simon Guest closed the front door of his purpose built curate's house and began his walk to church. He made his way down Blackbird's Hill, passing some council houses on his left and a small housing estate on his right. At the bottom of the hill, he turned left into the old part of the village. Here and there along the side of the road, were timber-bricked cottages, with the odd, larger house set back behind walled gardens. There was a post office that doubled as a general store and a sixteenth century pub with ancient beams and rugged walls. Further along on the same side was a path leading to some woods: the property of Sir Lionel and Lady Wilham, owners of Chinkton Manor.

Crossing the road, he sauntered over the large village green trim now with hawthorn bushes, red dabbed with fruit and the last remaining blackberries of the season. Towards the back, were lanky oaks, leaves half-fallen and beech and willow soaked in early morning dank and mist. Further along and to the side of the green, he came across four adjoining Tudor cottages and glancing up at one of the bedroom windows, saw a young woman watching him. Their eyes met briefly before she moved away. On he went, taking the footpath that led round the back of the green. Behind tall, stately yews stood the Norman church of St James. The clanging of a single bell summoned the parishioners to worship and along the grass verge, were an encouraging number of parked cars. Simon recognised

Lady Wilham as she walked briskly and purposefully down the church path. The last time they had met was at his interview. Simon liked her. In her late forties, he supposed and good looking too. A bit formidable perhaps, but pleasant nonetheless.

He glanced at his watch: eight fifty five. God! He was late.

'Dawdling again?' he could hear his mother say. 'Head in the clouds, as usual?' Simon ran the last few yards to the vestry.

⌀⌀

'Take and eat this in remembrance that Christ died for thee, and feed on Him in thy heart by faith with thanksgiving,' intoned George, administering a wafer of bread to each communicant as they knelt, heads bowed, at the altar rail.

The verger's wife said, 'Thank you, Rector,' as he placed a wafer of bread onto the palm of her hand. She always said, 'Thank you, Rector,' and it annoyed him intensely. The words broke his sense of occasion. George was a traditionalist, a partisan to the 1662 *Book of Common Prayer.* He loved and respected its formality and as neither the congregation, nor the Parochial Church Council raised any objections to its continued use, could see no reason for disbanding it in favour of its more modern counterparts.

Sheila, waiting her turn at the chancel, observed her husband's pronounced stoop. It reflected a malaise; a vague discontent that contrasted sharply with the new curate's straight backed, handsome, testament of youth. She was not, she thought sadly, a good rector's wife: had, she supposed, provided George with less than adequate support over the years of their long, up until now, surprisingly happy marriage. Solitary by nature, she had always felt a little threatened by village life and all its permutations.

As Lady Wilham knelt, straight backed at the communion rail, Sheila noticed her shiny-soled shoes: another new pair. She glanced with shame at her own serviceable navy blue courts; loose fitting, shapeless, stretched with age, the result of weekly treks to and from the church over wet rectory grass.

It was sometimes hard not to be envious of Beatrice – or Bea, as friends knew her: so smart, so self-contained, popular and nice. Lionel had been in the Shetlands seven months now and yet his wife carried on as usual, involving herself in village affairs and coping with the manor as though he were still there. It just wasn't Bea's style to moan.

The blessing over, George moved to the chancel steps and addressed the congregation. 'Before you all leave,' he said, 'I should like to welcome our newly ordained curate, Simon Oliver Guest. You are doubtless aware that in a parish like ours, small though it is, there is much work to be done. Whilst hoping to remain your rector for a few years yet, I welcome the help and support of our new priest.' There followed murmurs of approval and Simon felt himself blush furiously. 'I hope,' George finished, 'that you will welcome him into your homes and into your hearts.'

Nods, smiles, a final processional hymn, and the service was over.

'Well,' said George, as the two of them waited in the porch to greet the congregation on their way out, 'How did you enjoy your initiation ceremony? Not too gruesome, I hope?'

Simon laughed. 'I just hope that I passed muster.'

'I'm sure you did. Don't you agree, Charles?'

The churchwarden, on hand to collect the hymnbooks, gave Simon a cursory nod. He did not approve of lateness. 'You haven't forgotten the bell ringer's meeting next Thursday, Rector?' he said, pointedly changing the subject.

'No, I haven't forgotten, Charles.' There was an edge to George's voice and an undisguised relief at seeing Lady Wilham next in the queue of people waiting to meet their new curate. 'Good morning, Bea. Here's one introduction I don't have to make. You two have met already.'

She shook Simon vigorously by the hand. 'When you came to look us over.'

'Rather the other way round, I think, Lady Wilham.'

'Call me Bea.' She beamed, showing even, white teeth. 'All my friends do, and I count you as one already.'

'Thank you, I will.'

'So, do you like our village?'

'Very much. I passed by your woods this morning. A shame you can't see the manor from the village.'

'Come and see it now, if you like. There's no Matins this morning, and it's a lovely walk, and a lovely morning.' She placed a hand over her mouth. 'I'm so sorry, you probably want to get home for breakfast and some peace and quiet.'

Simon laughed. 'Not at all. I'd like to come.'

A few minutes later they were crossing a stile at the back of the churchyard and taking a footpath across a low-level tract of grassland. In the distance Simon could see the limestone hills and in front of him, set in a slight hollow, where well kept lawns and shrubs blended with the surrounding woodland, stood the manor: an Elizabethan house of brick and stone, gauzed by a veil of fine, morning mist.

Climbing the ha-ha that separated the field from the manor's garden, they paused to rest on an old, rusty iron seat placed beneath a sweet chestnut tree. Here, ripe nuts, some still wearing their spiny coats, lay scattered around the bole. The bark was old and tinged grey, its surface cracked with deep spiralling fissures. The branches bore leaves, some paling to yellow, others already beaming gold.

'We have our ancestor, Sir Egbert Wilham to thank for this,' said Bea, turning up the collar of her camel haired coat and giving the trunk a pat. 'He planted it in the eighteenth century and it's still going strong, as you can see.'

It must be good knowing about your relatives, your ancestors,' said Simon, laying a crumpled carrier bag at his feet. 'Gives you a sense of belonging, doesn't it?'

'I suppose it does, yes. Sir Egbert was second baronet of the manor, and rumour has it that his wife haunts the house.'

'A family ghost? Marvellous.'

'It's not always marvellous, believe me.'

'No?'

'No. We're having some trouble with poltergeist activity at the moment. China breaking without rhyme or reason. Oh, I know it all sounds so ridiculous, far fetched. The staff are getting quite edgy and spooked out about it. Their main worry, I think, is that I blame them for the accidents. I don't, of course but try convincing them. They're afraid to touch anything of value now. Nothing much gets dusted anymore. It's affecting their work and moods; all very unsettling, not to mention expensive.'

Simon, who had never considered any ghost apart from the Holy One, looked at her fascinated.

She frowned. 'I don't, of course, go along with the paranormal, I'm far too practical for that. There has to be a logical explanation. I caught Birdie, our housekeeper, crying her eyes out the other day. It really is most distressing.'

'I'm sorry. It obviously distresses you.'

'All of us.'

'Is Sir Egbert buried in Chinkton Green?'

'Yes, he is. He, his wife and son are all buried in St James' churchyard. There is a tomb at the side of the vestry, but it's covered in lichen, so you can't really make out the inscription. I really must clean the stone sometime and get the railings fixed.' She seemed distracted all of a sudden and now stood up, her manner suddenly abrupt. 'Come on. I'll show you the house.'

'How is your husband getting on in the Shetland Isles?' Simon asked, as they walked briskly across the lawn.

'Lionel's fine. You know, I can't believe it's over seven months since he answered that advertisement in *The New*

Scientist.'

'It's research work that he's doing, isn't it?'

'Wild life, birds mainly.' Bea picked a twig lying on the grass and began peeling the bark. 'I had a dickens of a time persuading him to go for the interview. It's his first real job outside this estate.' She paused. 'You know, Lionel had to give up everything to care for this place.'

'Really?'

'We met at university – were both reading Biology. Ridiculously in love, we were. Still are. Corny, isn't it?' She softened, smiled, and Simon glimpsed a young girl, attractive and vibrant. 'Then four years later, as Lionel was completing his Masters, his father died suddenly of a heart attack and Lionel was left with the horrendous task of putting this estate to rights. The manor had gone to pot and the land was in dire need of reconstruction. There was very little money and masses to do, so his future career was put on hold. He came down from university – had to. We got married three months after that. His future now lay here, with the manor, and I have to say that he has made a damned good job of it.'

'You both have, by the looks of things.'

'The farming potential is very good here. We've rich pasture and arable land, plus of course, the wood that we work for coppicing and timber. Lionel decided not to renew the farm tenancies but to turn farmer himself. And so we employed this marvellous manager who taught Lionel more or less everything there is to know about this place. He really had his finger on the button, that man. It was largely thanks to his organisational skills that we were able to recoup some of the money lost when Lionel's father was alive.'

'Some achievement,' said Simon, looking around him in admiration. 'And this garden's just incredible.'

'It's at its best now – not so lovely in the winter, of course. We had such a dry summer in the Midlands this year. That's why the change is early.'

'That's purple sage, isn't it?' Simon asked, pointing to a

mass of foliage tucked in by large, voluptuous shrubs and overhanging trees whose fuchsin tints garnered the lawn. A rage of autumnal colour, crimson charged with gold, claret and green, chestnut and tan, merged in unrelievable glory. Leaves, some already frizzed and browned, others pellucid and veined lay on grass and under foot while autumn crocuses scattered the lawn, their little white stems reaching hungrily for the sun. The manor was splendid too. The brick work was covered in brilliant *Virginia Creeper* and thick, red *Pyracantha* faced flower beds of low growing *Asters, Golden Rod, Chinese Lantern, Dahlias* and *Goldsturm*.

'The garden is my territory,' said Bea, unashamedly proud. 'I planned, pruned, and replanted all of this, with help, of course. Oh,' she laughed, 'I nearly forgot to mention the maze, my pride and joy. Simon looked around him. 'You can't see it from here. It's on the other side of the garden, but it's quite a feature, partly because of its age and size.'

'Sir Egbert again?'

She laughed. 'A bit of a benefactor, was Sir Egbert.' And digging her hands deep into the pockets of her coat, 'I love this manor.'

'I'm not surprised. Your hard work has certainly paid off.'

'Thank you.' Her smile was warm, appreciative. 'Look,' she said, as they neared the house, 'why not come round for lunchtime drinks? I'll ask George and Sheila.' Simon was about to say that he would love to, when a short plump, woman came running, breathless, out of the house and up to were they stood. 'What's the matter, Birdie?' Bea, her face now flushed and tense.

'There's been an accident, madam.'

'Anyone hurt?'

Birdie shook her head, looking at Simon, as though for inspiration. 'It's the *Meissen*. The figurine on the hall table, madam.'

'What about it?'

'It's broken.'

'Broken!'

'Smashed, madam.'

'But that was a wedding present. Oh, God! No! How did it happen?'

'Well, that's just it, madam. We don't know.'

Ø Ø

When Adelina saw what she had done, her first thought was to leave, to get as far away from the manor as possible. But where could she go? This was her home: every nook, every cranny explored, remembered and loved.

She tried to compose herself, reason things out; give herself another chance. But as she gazed transfixed at the shattered pieces; the beautiful Meisson figure, the shepherd and shepherdess smashed beyond repair, she knew that her chances were running out.

She left the hall then and made her way towards the library, her passage painfully slow and marked by many pauses and sighs. When she finally reached the long, oak-panelled room, with its many books lining the walls, there was someone there before her. A stranger too. He was sitting to the right of the fireplace, cross-legged in a mulberry coloured chair browsing through one of the calf bound books and turning each tissue thin page with meticulous care.

Adelina turned to go. She needed her time, her space: did not feel like being sociable today, of all days. But something about the way he held his head, the slim line of his body and the furrow of his brow, made her pause and stare. Sensing her presence, he raised his head and smiled.

'Thomas!' she gasped. Could it be? Surely not. But the manner in which he rose from his chair and glided towards her, the glint in his eye and the measure of his smile left her in no doubt. 'After all these years, Thomas. I cannot believe it!'

He smiled, at once sympathetic. 'Such sadness, that day

of your passing. I remember it well.' He paused. 'Influenza, was it not?'

'Pneumonia, Thomas.'

'Ah! Of course, of course. Pneumonia. Very sad.'

'And you, Thomas?'

'Me? The Ague.'

'Ah!'

He extended a slim arm, fringed with deep, white cuffs. 'Come! Adelina. Let us not dwell on such morbid things. Let us instead dance *The Menuet de la Cour*.'

She bowed her head. 'I cannot.'

'Cannot?' His eyes widened. 'But I taught you the dance myself.'

'I cannot glide, Thomas.'

'Cannot glide?'

'That is what I said.' Why must she repeat such humiliations.

'Cannot glide,' he reflected, drawing out the words and then briskly, 'See now, see how I glide.' And he coasted over to the library window, turned and beamed. Adelina sighed. He was as arrogant and vain as ever. Yet had she possessed a heart, it would have been thumping nineteen to the dozen. 'Have you forgotten, Thomas?' she said.

A tilt of the head, a hint of a smile, 'Your feet?'

She nodded.

'No better?'

'Worse.'

'I am sorry to hear that.'

'I have no control over them, none whatsoever. Sometimes I travel at horrendous speeds, at others hardly at all. Her voice faltered, grew faint. 'And I break things.' Thank heaven her feet were hidden beneath her long, silk, pocket-hooped skirt. Yet even as they stood ghost to ghost, she knew that he remembered their grossness and her shame. That he still held memories of those days when she and Sir Egbert had played host to the county set and led the dancing for two hours at a time. All would be well, Adelina told herself over and over. Tonight she would not lean too heavily to the left or to the right, would point her toes just so; smile, look up, flirt a little, laugh. Be the perfect hostess.

At eight o'clock there was country dancing. The break was at nine, when tea and light refreshment briefly suspended her misery. The interval over, there was a change of partners and off they went again. She counted the hours, counted the minutes. On the first stroke of eleven, the orchestra ceased playing, often in the middle of a bar, as though they too could not wait to finish. Then there was the fetching of cloaks, the thanks, the kisses, the coaches and chairs, the torches, the leave taking and finally the merciful silence. Next the trail up to bed, the undoing of stays, the removal of slippers, the swollen feet. And finally bed, blessed bed. But then came the dreams: sniggering ladies, pinched toes, forgotten steps, hidden blushes, pleading headaches. Awful! Quite, quite awful! But Thomas never gave up on her. Daily, they practised, *The Minuet, The Pavan and Galliard*. The little progress she made was largely thanks to him. Her mother had tried to reassure her, for was she not blessed with soft, gentle grey eyes; a pretty face and engaging smile? But what use were fair looks, if you could not dance? Better to catch the pox and suffer disfigurement than be lubberly and unpolished on the dance floor. Why, Lady Drool had been covered with pox marks and yet was never short of a partner. No. A pretty face could not compensate for large, unwieldy feet. Thomas was the only one who had understood. And even he had grown impatient at times. But she had come to rely on him: his encouragement; the promise that one day, she would master the skill – perhaps be the best dancer in the county. But that day never came.

Thomas had returned to his seat and crossed long, lean legs. 'You must cease fretting,' he said. 'Many ghosts take years to perfect The Glide, you know.'

'But I have already waited years, Thomas. I need to

travel, to be mobile. And yet here I am stuck in this manor, alone, without a single soul-mate to keep me company.' She eyed him sharply. 'And where is my husband, you may ask? Why do you not, Thomas? Not one enquiry have you made about Sir Egbert.'

'Well, I ...'

'He is not here, you know. Never has been. The poor soul is haunting the wrong house, he is stuck in some dreadful pub in the north of England. It is monstrous!'

'Most distressing,' Thomas replied, inspecting his nails, 'And the landlords, what of they?'

'They are ghastly! Quite the worst!'

'Yes, yes. I am sorry.'

'You know them?'

'Mm? Well, sort of. The Haunting Association. They told me.'

'You work for The Haunting Association?'

'Most certainly not,' he replied shortly. 'I am freelance; like to be my own boss.'

'So, what *do* you do, Thomas?'

'Oh this and that, you know,' he returned, brushing a cobweb from his silk breeches. 'A little guiding, here, a little guiding there; and I offer some counselling to all those poor lost creatures who do not know what has hit them once they have reached the other side. On occasion I have reason to liaise with the association on behalf of a client, do you see. And so my reason for being here is in part to offer *you* my help, Adelina.' His eyes glistened. 'But I wanted, in any case, so much to see you again.'

'Well, you have left it long enough, Thomas, I must say.' She, outwardly peeved, inwardly delighted. 'Egbert should not be marooned in that God forsaken place. Do you know the cheek of it, those dreadful landlords claim him as their resident ghost? They make money out of him you know, yes.'

'I had heard something of the kind.'

She moved closer. 'Tell me, Thomas, have you seen him – Sir Egbert?' And when he did not answer, 'Well, have you?'

'One hears things,' he replied, avoiding her eye. 'Word gets about. He is not a happy ghost, that I do know.'

'Well, I know that too, and I have asked The Haunting Association to do something, help him, but they say it is beyond their power to relocate him. According to them, only human intervention can move him on.'

Thomas sighed. 'Yes, I see. And your son, Maurice – where is he?'

'Maurice is another worry.'

'He is not here with you either, I take it,' said Thomas looking around as though he half expected him to appear.

Adelina shook her head. 'Maurice is not here by choice. He chooses to haunt the local Biddlington Theatre, instead of staying here with me. I wish he would come home, I really do, but he would be bored stiff in this old house with only his unhappy mother to keep him company. And he is set on that place.' She gave a wan smile. 'Do you remember Thomas, when he was a child, how he used to enjoy dressing up and acting in his own little plays?'

'I do. Indeed I do.'

'He wanted to become a professional actor, you know, but his father forbade it.'

'Yes, well that was understandable. After all, it was unfitting for a man of his class, landed gentry, to take up a theatrical career. You know that. It would have been most unsuitable. People would have talked.'

'Well anyway,' she sniffed, 'relations between him and his father were never the same after that. It is all rather sad. The actors find Maurice a nuisance, you know.'

'How could they? Such a delightful young man.'

'Yes, but a head strong one. He gets in the way, do you see? Makes bogus appearances on stage, speaks the actor's lines for them and moves the props.' She chuckled. Naughty boy!'

'Are you able to visit him?'

'I try, I really do, to lend my support, but astral travel is so difficult for me, Thomas. I never know where I will end up.'

His eyes, brown and soft, held hers. 'Ah yes. It cannot be easy without your husband to keep you company.'

'Oh, Thomas, it is not.' She took a step towards him. 'It has been so long, Thomas. I thought I would never see you again. That you had forgotten me.'

'Never!' he said, taking her hand. 'Our short mortal time together was too precious to forget.'

She sighed. 'Egbert knew about us. You know that. Of course you must know that.'

He did not reply, but stretched out his hand and touched her face, stroked her aura. He cooed and kissed her. His hands caressed and soothed her. Gossamer-like thrills teased and tingled her ether, until ecstasy, culminated in one almighty shudder that lifted her four feet into the air.

'That was wonderful,' she moaned, while coming to rest at his side. 'Do it again, Thomas.' He adjusted his black beaded waistcoat. 'Not now, Adelina. I have not the time.'

'But you have all the time in the world.'

'That is where you are wrong, Adelina. My job requires a good deal of travelling: visiting clients and drumming up the business. Being self employed is not easy. I have to seek work. It does not always come to me. There is talk of another recession, you know.'

'Oh, for goodness sake, Thomas,' she snapped, turning her back and there followed a frosty silence. 'My feet are frozen,' she said at length, throwing him a sideways glance.

'Well, that is not unusual, you know, not in our state.'

'Mm. Well anyway, I do not like it. I hate the cold, always did. You are a ghost guide and a counsellor. Help me,' she pouted.

'Oh really, Adelina! You know as well as I do that we cannot always control our thermostats.'

'Do you think that the cold is hindering my glide? Answer me that.'

He closed his eyes and suppressed a sigh: more problems. He wished, oh, how he wished that he could harness his assets into something a little more enterprising. He had been at his present job too long: was engulfed by ghosts who had little or no chance of sorting themselves out: Lost ghosts, lonely ghosts, neurotic ghosts, displaced ghosts, cold ghosts, frightened ghosts, evil ghosts. The list was endless. He was drained, exhausted. In short, he had had enough. He wanted out.

'As I see it, Adelina,' said Thomas, trying not to show his irritation, 'you have three distinct problems: One, you desire your husband's return, two, you feel the cold and three, you cannot glide, at least not properly with due control. Very well. Which one of these problems shall we tackle first?' He raised a politic finger. 'I cannot stay long, now.'

'The cold, that is what we should tackle first. I cannot function properly when freezing cold, now can I?'

'Very well.'

She smiled, and settling herself on a footstool, looked up at him fondly.

'The spectral chill that we feel,' began Thomas, gliding back and forth, 'is peculiar to our state and permeates our environment. We can however, feel less cold if we so wish. Indeed, it is within our power to feel warm. So how do we accomplish this? You must first warm a mortal of your choice: a human being who suffers from the cold. Thus from them you will extract the heat that you require.' He coasted to the far end of the library, rose into the air, hovered next to a row of books on tropical diseases, and gave a loud resounding sniff. Moments later, the room, normally a little fusty, was filled with the sharp smell of apples.

Adelina jumped. Something strange was happening to her, her memory was zipping back in time, right back, way back to when she was a child: to orchards, to boughs fruit burdened and to apple picking pleasure. Ah, the smell of it all brought tears of nostalgia to her eyes. But then it faded but its transient magic was replaced with the pungency of damask roses. Ah, the sweet smell of those pink blowsy blooms. 'Don't fade, don't fade,' she cried, but over this now returned another smell, the familiar smell of eau de Cologne – the redolence of a lifetime's use: A little dab behind the ears, at the throat and in her square laced handkerchief. Wonderful! In seconds she had tumbled back to an essentialness that even the cobwebs of time could not erase. And then slowly, luxuriously, heat began to seep through her toes, up through her back and stomach, right up to the top of her head.

'It is your memory, Adelina,' said Thomas, seeing her face soften with pleasure. 'Nothing more than your memory, remember that. Your recollections of apples, roses and eau de Cologne are pleasing, and pleasant reminiscences can empower us with warmth.'

'Really?'

'Really!'

'Well,' said Adelina grinning broadly. 'That is easy enough. I will recall sweet memories all the while and be forever warm. Most pleasing.'

'That was a mere teaser, Adelina, a small experiment to show you how it works. In our fragile state we need to link with mortals before we can experience more permanent benefits. Just as you will need to make mortal contact before Egbert is released from the clutches of Doris and Harold, so you will need to make mortal contact to feel permanently warmer.'

'I see,' said Adelina, who did not see at all.

'As I said earlier, you need to choose a human who feels cold. Not physically cold, but emotionally chilly.'

'Do you know of anyone, Thomas?'

He thought for a moment. 'There is the Rector of St James. Yes, yes, he might do. Now, there is a man who feels distinctly chilly. His wife cannot abide his snoring and sleeps in a separate chamber to ensure her rest. An otherwise happy marriage is marred by this vile habit. In addition, he has a crisis of faith. I may remedy that at some point; in the meantime, you can get to work.'

'I do not understand,' said Adelina, an edge to her voice,

'What, exactly, am I meant to do?'

'Visit him when he is relaxed: while he is taking an afternoon nap, for instance. Augment your presence by introducing into his room, into his nostrils, one or two of the aromas you have just experienced. By doing this you will acquaint his subconscious with sweet nostalgia: memories of such intensity he will not fail to reap the benefits. Hey presto! He feels happier, you feel warmer.'

There was the sound of approaching footsteps. Thomas glanced nervously towards the door. 'We must finish now.' And even as he spoke his figure began to fade, to grow smudgy around the edges.

'Do not go Thomas. Not yet. Not now when things are getting interesting.'

'I must!' His voice was faint.

'But you promised to teach me, The Glide,' she begged, clinging to his breeches. 'When do I get my gliding lesson?'

'Cease your tugging, Adelina,' he said, shaking her off, 'it weakens my electro-vital. You have plenty to be getting on with. I will teach you The Glide next time.'

'Please, please stay with me.' Now only one stockinged foot remained. 'Stay, at least until Egbert returns.'

But there was no reply. Thomas had gone.

two

'I've no objection to our church fete being held at the manor, George. All I ask is that women don't plough up my lawn with their wretched high heels.' Bea, her voice unusually edgy, snapped shut her cigarette case.

Two Springer spaniels sat on the far side of the room growling at an old wooden rocking chair. Occasionally they stopped, and wagged their tails. Simon sat sipping his orange juice and wished they would shut up. He glanced at his watch, one o'clock. If he left now, he might manage to book a quick flight at that flying club he'd joined; bit of luck that – finding Longbourne Airfield on his doorstep. Now that he had gained his private pilot's license, he couldn't wait to practise solo flying. He drained the rest of his drink. Thank God for dear, departed Uncle Justus and that small legacy he had left him. Not a fortune, but just enough for him to indulge his favourite hobby.

'Another drink, Simon?' asked Bea. 'Something stronger perhaps?'

'Not for me, thanks.' He sprang to his feet. 'I must be off.'

'I'd better be making tracks as well, Bea,' said George, following suit. 'Sheila will have kept lunch, and I've a baptism at four.'

'Before you leave, George,' said Bea, 'we need to sort out this fete thing. By the way, you know Barnaby's leaving me?'

'Your butler?'

'He's off to warmer shores apparently.'

'Ah, sorry to hear that. Have you anyone to replace him?'

'I'm interviewing Freddie Pearson tomorrow. You know the Pearsons?'

George nodded. 'Indeed yes. Very good churchgoers – his parents are, at any rate. Maureen organises the flower rota and Freddie cuts our grass. So,' he laughed jovially, 'you're planning to poach Freddie from us, are you?'

'I hear he's looking for a job, that's all.' Bea, normally quick to spot humour, appeared unusually tense. 'Shut up dogs!' she roared and Simon jumped. The dogs, tongues lolling, stretched out on the floor: eyes doleful, heads resting on paws.

'Poor Freddie,' said George, ignoring the sudden outburst. 'He hasn't had much luck with jobs. He was made redundant from the garden centre in Pemberley, not long since. I'm sure he'll prove a reliable worker.' And as Bea ushered Simon to the door, 'Evensong, early as you can, please. The rest of our flock will be eager to meet their new curate.'

'I'll be there,' said Simon, giving a salute.

'Tope! Brill! Leave that rocking chair alone,' Bea ordered, and the dogs skidded across the wooden floor, to her side.

It was then that Simon saw her. There, on that same seat, swaying back and forth sat a woman: a woman wearing a long green dress, a white modesty piece, and an undress mob cap. She looked at him for a moment, smiled and vanished. He opened his mouth to speak, but no sound came. A ghost? Ridiculous! Pull yourself together man! There were no such things.

'You've gone quite white, Simon. Are you all right?' asked Bea touching his arm. Should he tell her – warn her perhaps? No, she would probably think him crackers – that he was letting his imagination run riot – hardly a good first impression.

'Couldn't be better,' he chirruped, relying on his acting skills to see him through. But as he followed her out of the drawing room, down the corridor towards the front door, he sensed that she knew.

Ø Ø

'Is that you, George?' called Sheila from the kitchen.

'Yes, dear.'

'I thought you might have stayed for lunch.'

'Of course not. Don't be silly. Not without you.'

'Well, you've been so long, the lamb has shrivelled to nothing. Do you want it?' Trying not to sound reproachful.

'Yes, please. I'm sorry I'm so late.' He put an arm round her shoulder. Felt her stiffen. 'You should have come, you know. Bea's all right. She doesn't bite.'

Sheila didn't answer; instead watched George sit at the table and stab away at the remainder of the meat. A piece skidded across his plate leaving a snail-like trail of gravy on the linen tablecloth.

'I thought perhaps we could take a holiday soon,' she said, resisting the temptation to clean up the mess. 'We need a break. What about our going to my sister's in Windermere? Anne's written to say they're off to France for one week in November. We could house-mind for them.' She stared pensively at the stained cloth. 'It's yoghurt for pudding – want some?'

'What? Oh, no thank you – just coffee.'

'Kettle's already boiled. You're miles away, George.'

'So are you.' He patted the seat beside him. 'Come and sit down.'

'What do you think about that holiday then?' she said, joining him.

'Mm. It would be nice. But we'll have to wait and see how Simon settles first. I need to know that he can be left in charge.'

'I'll write to Anne and say a provisional yes, then?' she nudged.

'All right, but when I've checked my diary.'

'I thought Simon came across well during the Eucharist.' She felt encouraged by his positive response. 'He has a clear speaking voice and it carries well.'

'He has indeed. Yes, I like him too, it's just that ...'

'What?'

'He seems a bit scatterbrained, that's all.'

'In what way?'

'He was late arriving for the service. When I say late, I mean that he made it with five minutes to spare. Charles was furious and let him know it. You know what he's like.' Sheila pulled a face. 'Simon needs to understand that taking a church service is not the same as catching a bus. As priests, it's important that we have time to compose ourselves before celebrating Holy Communion, or any other service for that matter. If it happens again, I'll have to have strong words.'

'You're right, of course.'

'And another thing,' said George, getting up to make his coffee. 'He arrived in the vestry carrying a *Marks and Spencer's* carrier bag. It appears that he keeps his vestments in a *Marks and Spencer's* carrier bag. Can you believe it? His surplice looked quite crumpled when he dragged it out.' He poured boiling water into his cup. 'There's something almost artless about him, d'you know?'

Sheila laughed. 'He's very young, George. Give him a chance.'

'He's young, yes. But surely to goodness you'd think that he'd have a proper case for his vestments.'

'Young people travel light nowadays.'

'Don't make excuses for him, Sheila. It may be a village, but the parishioners won't stand for sloppiness. A carrier bag,' he muttered, taking his coffee and walking to the door. 'You don't mind if I drink this in the study?'

She suppressed a sigh. 'Fine. I'll get stuck into the Sunday papers.'

'We'll have a nice break away I promise, as soon as we can.'

'I hope so. What time will you be back?'

'Around five. Shouldn't be any later. Save me a cup of tea.'

George sank heavily into his armchair and gazed vacantly through the study window at their rambling, unkempt rectory garden, luckily redeemed by several large domed beeches. He sighed heavily. Estranged, that's how he felt, as though he had been plunged into voluntary exile. Where, if anywhere, did he fit into the order of things? He was married, yet didn't feel married. He was a clergyman and yet had doubts about his faith; and if he had doubts about his faith what was he doing masquerading as rector of St James? His thoughts grew mistier, his eyes grew heavier. They closed. He slept: the deep, dreamless sleep of blissful oblivion and when he awoke felt revitalised alert. He sat up, looked about him – had the strangest feeling of being watched. Sheila? He turned, half expecting to see her standing there. The Victorian mantle-piece clock chimed the half-hour. Time to go.

George took his cassock and stole out of the cupboard then stopped. His nostrils twitched. Apples? Was that apples he could smell? Was Sheila baking a pie for Simon this evening? She normally bought that sort of thing from *Sainsbury's*. As he put on his cassock, slowly placed the white stole around his neck, the smell grew stronger, pricking his nostrils, watering his mouth. It reminded him of his mother's pies, those thick pastry tarts deep filled with fruit and peppered with cloves; their flower buds peeking through the apples, brown and sharp.

He rushed out of the study. 'Sheila!'

'I'm in the drawing room, reading.'

'Oh.' His voice dropped in disappointment. 'I thought perhaps you were baking.' He stood in the doorway watching her leaf through the pages of *The Sunday Times*.

'What is it?' She didn't look up.

'That pie smells done to me.'

'What pie? What are you talking about? I can't smell any pie.'

'But ...'

'George, shouldn't you be at the baptism by now?'

Without answering, he turned heel and marched down the passage to the kitchen; opened the oven door and looked inside. But the oven was empty. He marched into the larder. Here he was almost knocked back by the smell. Frantically he searched the shelves: flour, butter, packets of cereal, a half-eaten chicken – the usual provisions bought at the local supermarket, but there was no apple pie. He stopped. His heart paced, he felt queer. Not ill, but vibrant, charged, as though a torch had been switched on in his head. 'Sheila! Sheila,' he called. Come here!'

'There,' he announced, as she wandered into the larder. 'Now you can smell it.'

'I can smell damp. Will that do?' She glanced impatiently at her watch. 'You're going to be late, George.'

'All right, all right, I'm going.' He made his way back to the hall, put on his overcoat and left the house.

Sheila returned to the drawing room and glancing through the window, caught sight of George waking across the lawn. There was something odd about him, something different. A spring to his step, a buoyancy she hadn't seen in years, not since they were first married.

The doorbell interrupted her thoughts. It was Freddie.

'I can't do your garden tomorrow morning, Mrs Pym. Sorry, I've got to go to the manor. Afternoon okay?'

'Yes, I'm sure it is. You've just missed George, he's gone to take a baptism.'

Freddie put his head round the door. 'Mm, smells good.'

Sheila looked at him sharply, 'What do you mean, smells good?'

'Apple pie is it?'

'No.'

'Oh.'

'There are no apples here, Freddie.'

'Sorry.' He was only trying to be friendly.

'Look, can you spare a minute?' And before he had a chance to object, Sheila had whipped him inside, marched him down the passage and into the kitchen. 'Now,' she said, 'Can you smell apples in here?'

He paused. Sniffed the air. 'Yep.'

'And in here?' Marching him into the larder.

'Phew! I'll say.'

'What sort of apples?'

'*Bramleys*? Could it be?'

'How on earth do you know?'

'I've worked with fruit trees and that, at the garden centre.'

'It's really weird. George could smell the apples too, but I can't. Why can't I?'

He shrugged. How was he to know?

'Do you think it might be damp?'

'The smell? Damp? It's nothing like damp.' Cor, she'd a real problem with her nasal passages. 'Can't you smell it then, the apples?'

'No. And I haven't got a cold, either.'

'It's nothing like damp,' he repeated, inspecting the kitchen as though checking for fingerprints.

'It's so strange,' said Sheila, walking back to the hall. 'I don't understand it.'

'Strange things happen, Mrs Pym. Old houses sometimes retain scents from years back. It can get right into the woodwork and drawers.'

'Thanks, Freddie,' said Sheila, seeing him out, 'Sorry to have kept you.'

Freddie liked the crunching sound his feet made on the gravel, as he walked down the rectory drive; and the little piles of wet leaves at the side reminded him of soggy bran flakes. Roll on tonight! His heart thumped with pleasure at the thought of seeing Sophie: just a couple of hours now and he'd be with her. As he passed by the church, he noticed a woman standing on the porch steps. She was wearing a long green dress, with a close fitting bodice and a white cap with side pieces that dangled like spaniel's ears. Strange gear for a bride but brides wore anything these days. Hang on. The rector was taking a baptism, not a wedding. He stopped and looked more closely. She caught his eye, waved and beckoned. Perhaps she's come to the wrong church, he thought, as he walked towards her.

'Can I help you?' Was it his imagination, or did she smell fusty? Freddie was reminded of his old school textbooks, of dusty church hassocks, and old wet carpets. Perhaps she was a bag lady.

'Hello!' she said cocking her head to the side.

'The rector's taking a baptism,' shouted Freddie. 'But you can go into the church if you want to and watch the service, he won't mind.'

'I have already seen the rector, my dear. It is you I want.'

A stab of alarm. 'Me?'

The woman swayed. Drunk, was she?

'Let's go into the church,' he urged, wishing he hadn't stopped by. 'It's warmer in there. And you can tell me where you live.'

'There is no need for that. I know perfectly well where I live, young man.'

'What do you want then?' His manner gruff now to hide his nerves.

'I want your help.'

'Help?' Freddie swallowed. She stretched out her hand to touch him. He drew back sharply.

'Hello Mrs Figgot,' he called nervously, as mother and baby emerged from the church. She was wearing a straw hat with a large pink rose on the front. 'Had your baby christened then?'

'Deidre? Yes, lovely service too. How's Sophie?' Mrs Figgot cut Sophie's hair.

'Fine thanks.'

'Mrs Figgot!' The rector, breathless, hurried to her side, his surplice flapping in the breeze. 'May I compliment you on your hat? It is quite charming.'

'Well, thank you,' she said, flushing.

'May I ask where you acquired the rose?'

'The rose?'

'On your hat.'

'The rose came with it.'

'I wonder,' he said, eyeing it steadily, 'If I might smell it?' She stepped back in alarm. 'It hasn't got no smell.'

'All right, vicar,' cautioned Mr Figgot, moving alongside his wife. 'One sniff and that's it. Give us Deidre, then.'

'What for?'

'So as the vicar can smell your 'at.'

She handed him the baby, then inclined her head, as though about to receive a blessing. Freddie stared in amazement as the rector leant forward, and took long, intoxicating sniffs. The godparents giggled. They'd read about his sort in *The News of the World*.

'Do you know,' enthused George, 'the scent reminds me of damask roses. The fragrance takes me back to the many happy days I spent as curate in Leamington Spa.'

'That's nice.' Mrs Figgot shot a sideways glance at her husband, who was itching to get away to the pub.

What the heck's up with Mr Pym? thought Freddie. Was

he losing his marbles an' all? He was usually the brooding sort, was the rector. 'Deep,' that's how his mum described him. And why had no one noticed this woman in the funny green dress? Her get-up alone was enough to attract attention. Freddie took a deep breath and swung round, better to face her. But she was nowhere that he could see. She must have walked off while he wasn't looking. Phew! That was a relief. Right, he'd just do a quick check inside the church and then leg it. Once satisfied that she was nowhere in sight, he waved goodbye to the rector, now skipping happily towards the vestry; and ignoring a niggling sense of foreboding, left the church yard and made his way home.

Simon was lost. He was running low on fuel. It was five o'clock and he was still over fifty miles from base. He tried to select the emergency service's frequency but there was no response. He must be out of range. He had been flying in circles for the last fifteen minutes trying to get a position fix. His instruments gave him heading, height and air speed, yet he was damned if he knew where he was. There was a hell of a lot of low broken cloud, so much of the stuff he could barely see the ground. At all costs, he must keep to an altitude of one thousand feet. He peered through the windscreen. Where the hell was the motorway intersection? If he could spot that it would lead him to the lake that ran adjacent to Longbourne Airfield. Sweat trickled down the inside of his neck. His hands shook. He was going to die: he knew it. There was no way out of this. Useless – that's what he was. No sense of direction, no visibility, nothing. What was he doing in the air at all? He should never have stopped chatting to that girl in the airport bar at Long Pelham. But it wasn't every day he met a leggy blonde with a penchant for clerics. He had been pleased with his landing too, even if it had been a bit of a bouncer. Besides, it was good to stop off for a rest, take a look at the airfield and recharge his batteries.

'Oh, come on, for God's sake!' Simon sent a desperate prayer to the Deity that had about as much impact as his radio. 'Longbourne radio. Longbourne radio. This is Golf Papa Tango. I am lost. Repeat. I am lost. I am low on fuel and my radio is giving problems. Can you advise?'

Silence. He repeated the message. Nothing. A few crackles and pops and then a female voice: 'Papa Tango. This is Golf Foxtrot Alpha. Do you read me?'

'Roger, Golf Foxtrot Alpha,' Simon gulped. 'I read you.'

'Golf Papa Tango, where are you heading?'

'Longbourne Airfield.'

'I'm heading for Longbourne too. I read you clearly, so we must be fairly close. I'm flying a blue and white Cessna one seven two.'

'I'm flying a red and white Cessna one five two,' said Simon, unable to keep the joy out of his voice.

'Describe your surroundings please.'

'I think I'm over the River Wye. I can see a large church. Is it Hereford Cathedral? I must be at least fifty miles from Longbourne.'

'Golf Papa Tango. You are approximately west, south west of Longbourne. Can you see a service station from where you are?'

Simon affirmed: a square shaped service station, its neon lights acting as a beacon.

'Okay. Circle overhead the service station. Be with you in three minutes.'

Two minutes later Simon spotted the light aircraft that formatted to a distance of two hundred metres.

'Golf Papa Tango, I have you in my sight. Can you see me?'

'Affirm,' he breathed into his mic.

'Okay. I'm heading for Longbourne. Follow me please.'

Amen to that. He wasn't going to die after all, and with a bit of luck, might even make evensong.

Simon parked his Cessna on the tarmac. To be on terra firma was pure bliss. He rushed over to the plane that had brought him to safety. The pilot was tying down her aircraft, her face temporally hidden by a cloud of silky, blonde hair.

'I don't know how to thank you,' he said, speaking to the back of her head. She stood up, faced him. God! She was beautiful. Eyes, violet blue, her smile warm and open. He held out his hand. 'Simon Guest.'

'Liz Graham.' Her handshake was firm, confident. 'What was the problem?'

'I couldn't select the emergency frequency service.'

'Was that it? Come on. Let's take a look.' They walked over to where his plane was parked. 'I've seen you somewhere before, Simon, haven't I?'

'I don't think so.' He would remember if he had seen a stunning beauty like her.'

'Yes, of course!' She hesitated. 'I um, saw you this morning on your way to church.'

'Oh?' There had been no ravishing blondes in the congregation that was for sure.

'Well actually, I was staring out of the window of my cottage – admiring my country seat, and you walked by.'

He thought for a moment. Of course! 'So, you live in one of those highly desirable properties on the green.'

She nodded, grinning. 'I've just bought it – for weekends – to get away from the great metropolis. Your church bell wakes me every Sunday morning without fail.'

When they reached the Cessna, Liz opened the door, looked inside and examined the instruments. 'If you'd flicked this switch, it would have enabled you to turn the frequency dial. Here – see?' She pressed a switch on the dashboard. 'By flicking this, you could have altered your frequency interval to enable you to get the frequency you wanted.'

'I had no idea it was so simple,' he said, looking inside. I feel a complete prat.'

'Don't worry it happens to the best of us. Fortunately these pre-historic sets are on the wane. Anyway,' she said, shutting the aircraft door, and giving him that smile again, 'You will know for the future.'

Simon glanced at his watch. It was five thirty. A miracle! If he put a step on, he'd make evensong, and it was all thanks to this gorgeous woman.

three

'Two anyone?' shrieked the headwaiter, reviewing the queue. 'Can seat two!'

Freddie put up his hand. This was not how he had envisaged things at all. He shot Sophie a quick glance but queues and noise didn't seem to bother her. They were led to a table at the back of the restaurant right next to the kitchens. His heart sank. This was not right. It should be quiet and romantic, not full of noisy kids stuffing their mouths, and waiters yelling to each other.

'Is there nowhere quieter?' Freddie pleaded, as he seated Sophie furthest away from the swing doors through which staff thrust themselves with alarming velocity.

''Fraid not. You can see how it is.' The waiter placed two massive menus in front of them before weaving his way back to the front of the restaurant.

'You look lovely, Sophie.' Freddie tried to salvage some of his former optimism. 'Choose what you like.'

She scanned the menu. 'An Hawaiian pizza, please.'

'I'll join you. And two glasses of the house red?'

'Sounds good. I'm just slipping off to the ladies'. Won't be a tic,'

Freddie watched as she made her way towards the stairs. Her long, brown woollen frock clung softly to her figure accentuating the curves of her body. Someone scraped a chair across the tiled floor and he jumped. If only he could stop thinking about that weird woman he had met in the churchyard. Even now, hours later, the image was sharp in his mind: her dress, the smell, that unearthly quality he had witnessed before. Well, at least one thing had gone right: his interview at the manor had Sophie's seal of approval and that chuffed him no end. He looked at his watch. She was taking a while. The waiter came with their orders and looked questioningly at the empty chair. Then he spotted her, smiling at him from across the room. Relax man!

'Sorry to have been so long,' she said, 'only I've just had this lovely chat with the ladies' attendant.' She placed a napkin on her lap and looked about her. 'They really capture the atmosphere in here, don't they?'

'Do you think so?' Freddie was glad she didn't share his view. 'So what did you talk about then?'

'This and that. She lives in Chinkton Green and sounded ever so well to do; must have hit hard times to be working here. She was wearing fancy dress. Novel idea that, don't you think?'

'Eat up, Sophie, before it gets cold.'

She cut a small piece of pizza and popped it neatly in her mouth. 'That's rather a nice touch, don't you think, Freddie?'

'What is?' he said, retrieving a piece of sticky cheese from his chin.

'The fancy dress. Sort of unusual. Most restaurant toilets are pretty ordinary but this one is really pretty. The theme's green like in here and she was all in green too.' She stopped. 'Oh I nearly forgot; she said, she knew you.'

'Me?' Sophie hadn't touched her wine yet. He bet old Lady Wilham had some superb stuff.'

'Freddie – are you listening to me?'

'Of course I am.'

'What did I say then?' She stabbed him playfully with her fork.

'You said that she knew me.'

'That's right.'

'Well, I don't know any toilet attendant. Sophie, can we change the subject?'

'She met you this afternoon outside the church, that's what she said. You know, that's what I like about you, Freddie. You've always got time for everyone.'

Freddie put down his fork. 'St James? Outside St James' church?'

She nodded.

Freddie felt a chill run down his spine. 'Say again what she was wearing.'

'Fancy dress.'

'Yes, but describe it.'

'A long green, satiny dress that sort of stuck out at the sides.'

'Was she wearing a white cap thingy?'

'You do remember her, then. Yes, she was. What an eccentric lady! Still I rather like eccentric people, don't you?' She leaned across the table and took his hand. 'Are you all right? You look as though you've seen a ghost.'

'Sophie, I think we both have.'

'What?'

'I was walking home from the rectory this afternoon. I'd been to see Mrs Pym about changing my time tomorrow. I always do a bit of gardening there on a Monday. Well, as I passed by the church, I saw an old woman standing in the churchyard, beckoning to me. She was dressed in eighteenth century clothes like in a play they put on once at my school. What's it called?'

'*She Stoops to Conquer*?'

'That's the one.'

The waiter was back. 'Finished?'

Freddie nodded distractedly.

'Do you have a ladies' toilet attendant working here?' Sophie asked him.

'Not to my knowledge,' he replied, clearing their plates. 'The management barely runs to paying our wages let alone employing a toilet attendant. Dessert?' They settled on coffees.

'You do believe me, don't you?' said Sophie, after the waiter had gone.

'Of course I believe you.'

'She seemed to have trouble walking. Or perhaps she was drunk, but I don't think so.'

'That's her. The old girl was reeling about all over the place.'

'Don't exaggerate, Freddie.' She wrinkled her nose. 'Is someone eating apple pie? Smells good.'

'Well, have some. It's on the menu. I'll call the waiter.'

'No, coffee's fine, thanks.'

'Talking of apple pie reminds me.' Freddie wiped his mouth on his napkin. 'This afternoon, in the rectory, Mrs Pym asked me if I could smell apples in their study and in the kitchen. Funny thing was, I could smell them but she couldn't. It really bothered her as well.'

'Perhaps Mrs Pym doesn't have much of a sense of smell,' she chuckled. 'Now me, I can smell anything, especially my dad's socks.'

'Did the woman you met say anything else about our meeting?'

'Yes. She says she asked you for help.'

Freddie gave an involuntary shudder. 'I wonder if she's still there?'

'I could go and look, if you like.'

'No, I'd rather you didn't.'

'I don't mind, honest. I haven't seen a ghost before – least not a human one.'

'What do you mean, not a human one?' Freddie barely noticed their coffees being placed in front of them.

'I possess second sight,' said Sophie proudly. 'I see the spirits of departed animals.'

'Departed animals?'

'That's right. I was ten when my goldfish died. I placed the fish into an empty Smarty tube and buried it under the beech tree in our garden. Well, with Sigmund gone, that only left Alfonso and Henrietta swimming around in our fishpond.'

'They were goldfish too?'

She nodded. 'One morning, two weeks later, I went to feed them and there he was, back with the others, swimming around happy as anything.'

'But how do you know it was Sigmund?' Freddie signalled for the bill. 'Someone might have replaced the fish without your knowing. Anyway don't all goldfish look alike?'

'They do not.' She laughed, her eyes glistening. 'Sigmund was a black and white *Twinhead* and they are very rare.'

'Of course.' Right now he would agree with anything. Sophie was the most beautiful creature he had ever set eyes on. 'Have you seen any other animals from the spirit world?'

'Oh, yes. One rabbit, two dogs, a budgerigar and a horse.'

'That is a lot.' He leaned forward and popped an *After Eight* mint into her mouth.

'There's an awful lot of animals that have passed over,' said Sophie, her mouth full of chocolate. 'One day I'd like to do sittings for people so they can make contact with their pets.'

She was wonderful sitting there all flushed and enthusiastic, talking about a subject closest to his heart.

Sophie giggled. 'What you staring at?'

'Nothing.'

'Go on Freddie, say it.'

'Say what?'

'You think I'm daft.'

'No I don't.' Here was the perfect opening. It didn't matter now. He could tell her. They were two like minds. He took a deep breath. 'Sophie, I'm also –'

'Psychic? Yes, I know.'

'You know?' His voice rose in alarm. 'How do you know?'

'You have that look about you. Around the eyes.'

'Oh, thanks a lot. My dad's dead scared of that look.'

'No, it's nice, sort of dreamy, far away. I rather like it and it's nothing to be ashamed of – being psychic, I mean.'

He flushed. 'Sometimes, you know Sophie, I don't feel normal.'

'Heck! Who wants to be normal?' She took his hand. 'You and me, Freddie, we make a good team: me with the animals and you with the humans.'

'Since five, I've known I was different. I could see things others couldn't. It worried my folks.'

'Why should it? It didn't worry mine. Plenty of children are psychic.'

'It worried them because we had all these "lodgers" in the house.'

'Imaginary friends, do you mean? Well, that's normal enough.'

'Not imaginary friends, Sophie, ghosts. They came and went. I saw them with my own eyes, it was really weird. My folks didn't, of course. I was the nutter. They even considered taking me to see a child psychologist.'

Sophie laughed. 'They thought you were disturbed?'

'They still do. You know, our home was just an ordinary small, council house up north, but it must be one of the most haunted places in England.'

'You serious?'

'I'm serious, all right.'

He began telling her of his sightings and of his plan to one day write a book. It was wonderful to get it off his chest – to talk to someone who really understood. 'When I was twelve,' he said, 'I started having premonitions. That was really scary.'

'Why?'

'Because they were always nasty.'

'Nasty premonitions?'

'Death.'

She shuddered.

'Two uncles and one second cousin.'

'No!'

He nodded, enjoying her attention, the intent way she looked at him. 'The worst one was about my grandfather. He was a Yorkshire farmer – my mum's dad.'

'What happened to him?'

'He was eaten.'

'Eaten? You're joking!'

'By one of his pigs.'

'I didn't know pigs ate people.'

'This one did. It was huge, a huge hog weighing two hundred kilos: large, black, temperamental and unstable. We called him Bellygod. Anyway I predicated his end – my poor grandfather's that is. I felt pretty rough about it afterwards. I think my folks wondered about me more than ever after that: they kept me at arm's length, from then on.'

Sophie's eyes widened. 'You think they're scared of you?'

'Not scared exactly, more wary, perhaps.'

'That's sad, Freddie. Really sad.'

'Yeh. Well, anyway, my mother inherited some money from my grandfather, my dad got a transfer and we moved south to Chinkton Green. I think they wanted to get away from that council house and the area and start again. Maybe my parents thought things would change with the move. But I didn't change, that was the trouble. And they couldn't get away from me, could they?' He paused, looked into his coffee. 'My mother started going all religious.'

'You mean she prayed a lot?'

'He nodded. She goes to church every Sunday, and prays for me. Sometimes she takes my dad and they both pray. Can you imagine?'

'You must feel like you have a disease or something.'

'Yeh, something like that.' He looked at her levelly. 'You won't tell anyone of this, will you?'

'Of course I won't. But you must try not to mind. Rise above it. You possess a gift. Feel proud.'

He squeezed her hand. 'Thanks Sophie.'

The evening was mild, as they wandered arm in arm towards the car park. A harvest moon had settled overhead lending light to the half-timbered cottages that lined the streets.

'We'd better make a move,' he said, picking up speed. 'We've got six minutes before they lock the gates.'

They walked fast; passed the old market place and town hall, until turning the corner of Trellis Street, they came to Bricket Lane. Immediately in front of them stood the church, its simple eleventh century beauty illuminated against the sky. Freddie's old blue Cortina was parked in the far corner of the small adjoining car park. Shivering, he searched in his pocket for his car keys. It felt more like January than October. Funny, how the temperature had suddenly dropped.

'Someone walk over your grave, Freddie?'

'Oh, don't say that!' But his teeth chattered as he searched in his pocket for coins to feed the meter. Sophie walked to the car, drawing her coat around her for warmth as Freddie unlocked the passenger door, started the engine and began the drive back to Chinkton Green.

'Funny about that old lady,' mused Sophie. 'I mean, us both seeing her like that?'

'Yes, well perhaps we should both lay off those magic mushrooms for a bit.'

'I wonder what she wanted though? Must have been important for her to get in touch with us both.' She touched the dashboard. 'This a CB radio?'

'Yep. Once we're off this main road, I'll show you how it works, if you like. Do you feel any warmer?'

'Not really.'

He switched up the heating before turning left at the next junction. A couple of miles on, he turned into Crofts Lane, and stopped the car under a large beech. In the wider section of the lane, one or two other cars were parked. Freddie turned off the engine and the headlights. They said nothing. Held hands in the darkness. Freddie's heart thumped. A branch scraped across the car roof.

'It's very quiet,' Sophie whispered.

'Do you like the CBH radio then?'

She giggled. 'I haven't seen it properly yet.'

Freddie picked up the slim, rectangular box hanging on the dashboard. 'It's a nice bit of kit, don't you think? It only cost me forty quid with the aerial.'

'Let's get it to work – see if there's anyone out there.'

He twisted the channel selector, picked up the microphone and spoke into it. 'One four for a copy. Any breakers? Any takers? Is there anyone out there?' There was a lot of hissing and crackling. 'One four for a copy. Any breakers, any takers? Is there anyone out there?' Still nothing.

'Shall we leave it on, Sophie and try later?' And with hands shaking, he slowly turned her face towards his. The CB hissed softly in the background as he bent to kiss her.

Sophie suddenly pulled away. 'What was that?'

'What was what?' His dreamy response.

'Someone's trying to get through.'

'Is that all!' He pulled her close; kissed her long and hard.

'Mm, that's nice,' she whispered and was about to reach for his mouth a third time when, 'Listen!'

'What now? Really Sophie, where's your concentration?'

'Sh! A woman's voice. What's she saying? Speak into it, Freddie. Go on.'

'I've a better idea. Why don't we switch this thing off and climb into the back?'

'I want to know what she's saying. It was your idea. Remember?'

Freddie sighed and took hold of the mic. 'Breaker on the side, slide and crank it.'

'That's funny talk,' said Sophie. 'What's slide and crank it?'

'In CB language it means, "I want to join in a conversation. Come in and tell me your name".'

'Okay. Keep going.'

'Breaker, you are in the back of my box.'

'What does that mean?'

'It means that the voice is so weak, I can hardly hear. Oh, Sophie. Let's not bother. There are other things I'd rather be doing right now.' He drew her close and nuzzled his face in her hair.

'Wait! Did you hear that?'

'What?'

'She said something.'

'Hello breaker,' Freddie repeated. 'You are in the back of my box.'

A series of crackles and then, 'I left my box years ago and I have no wish to share yours.'

'Right!' announced Freddie, 'That's it. I'm turning this thing off.'

'Why?' protested Sophie, 'Just when we're through to someone, you want to turn it off.'

'Because it's a wind up, Sophie. You get them. Some crackpot.'

'No, wait. Ask her some more. Please.'

'Breaker, you there?' he bawled.

'There is no need to shout,' came the reply.

'Okay. Pick a window!'

'A what?'

'I said, pick a window, because you are in the back of my box.'

'How can I pick a window when I cannot see a window to pick?'

'Oh Freddie, stop teasing her. She doesn't understand. Here! Give me that thing.' Sophie took the microphone from his hand. 'What do I have to do?'

'Push the button and keep your finger on it while you're talking, and then let go of it when she answers.'

'Hello caller. Are you still there?' Sophie released the button.

'Yes, I am still here. Greetings to you, Sophie.'

She gasped. 'How do you know my name?'

'Because my dear, you told me your name this evening.'

Sophie grabbed Freddie's arm. 'It's her!'

'Now listen to me,' said the voice. 'We do not have long

and I am tired. I think that you and I will get along quite well, Sophie, but I sense some resistance from your friend. Do you think that he will be willing to talk to me?'

'Of course he will. You're not resistant are you, Freddie?'

He shook his head lamely.

'He says, he's not.'

'Very well. Now first, I must ask if you are both prepared to assist me?'

'Well, that depends,' said Sophie, who was nobody's fool and liked to be in full command of the facts. 'We need to know more about you first. Freddie says that he saw you earlier today, in St James' churchyard. I met you in the ladies at the Pizza Parlour and now you turn up on his CB. Why are you following us? And why are you in fancy dress?'

Freddie looked at her amazed. Really, there was no phasing the girl. Others would have run a mile or screamed in terror at the mere thought of being in this creature's company, but not Sophie.

'I've an idea,' he whispered. 'Give me the mic a minute. I'll just test her with a bit more jargon and then see if she'll meet us.'

'Meet us now?' said Sophie. 'It's much too late for that. You can't expect her to come out at this hour?'

'Why not? She probably does all her visiting at night. If she wants us that badly, she'll turn up.'

'Breaker,' he said, taking the mic, 'I'm square wheel at Crofts Lane. Do you want to come here for an eyeball?'

'An eyeball?' she snapped. 'I cannot produce such textural things.'

'Right, well you obviously don't understand. In plain English then: will you meet us? We are stationary in a parked blue Ford Cortina in Crofts Lane. Do you know Crofts Lane?'

More crackles and hisses.

'Caller, are you still there? Hello caller.' Freddie switched off the CB and returned it to the dashboard. 'The old girl's gone. Sorry, Sophie.'

'Oh come on, Freddie. Try some more.'

'She's gone, I tell you.' He ran a hand through his hair, straightened his tie and switched on the ignition. 'Better be getting back.' May as well abandon any further ideas of romance for the night.

The engine spluttered into life. Freddie checked for on-coming traffic in his rear mirror, gasped, did a double take and stalled the car. There, reflected in the glass was the woman he'd met outside the church. He swung round but there was nothing there. The back seat was empty but another check in the mirror confirmed she *was* there, bathed in a yellow light and staring straight at him.

'What is it?' demanded Sophie. 'What's the matter?'

'It's her. In the mirror.'

She leant over his lap. 'God! You're right.'

Freddie got out of the car.

'Where are you going?'

'I'm going to get to the bottom of this. Wind up your window and lock the door. I'll be back in a minute.'

He looked about him, but the moon was in cloud now and it was too dark to see anything much. Freddie checked his side mirrors front and back – nothing there. He began walking up the lane. There just had to be some logical explanation for this. But had there? Why was he getting so heated? He believed in ghosts, didn't he? And yet this latest incident had left him more unnerved than ever before. In the past, phantoms had come and gone but none had pursued him. Being followed by a ghost, if it was a ghost, was not a pleasant feeling. The moon emerged from cloud. Freddie recovered some of his nerve and walked towards a parked Range Rover. He knocked on the glass.

The window lowered a couple of inches. 'Yes?'

'Sorry to trouble you,' said Freddie feebly. 'But have you seen an elderly lady walk this way?'

'Lost your granny, have you? Push off, there's a good lad. I'm busy.'

A trail of female laughter followed him back to the car.

He climbed inside keeping his eyes firmly fixed on the dashboard. 'Is she still here, Sophie?' He wasn't going to chance another look in that mirror.

'Look Freddie, she wants our help that's all. Nothing wrong with that.'

'You've talked to her?' But before Sophie could answer …

'Greetings to you both!'

'Sophie!' Freddie hissed, sliding down into his seat. 'I've never spoken to a ghost before.'

'Yes, you have. You spoke to her on the CB.' She leaned across him to take a closer look.

'Sophie, my dear,' said the reflection, 'Use the mirror on your side. You will see me well enough. Freddie, I am sorry, if I frightened you, appearing as I did, without warning. Sometimes the mere thought of travel is enough to propel me to a destination at the most alarming speed. At other times I barely move at all. At all events I have to be careful.'

Freddie nudged Sophie. 'Ask her how she does it.'

'You ask her.'

'How did I manage to appear on your CB?'

Freddie chanced a quick glance. 'Yes, please.'

'Many things are possible in my state. But first, allow me to introduce myself. My name is Lady Adelina Wilham.'

'Are you related to Sir Lionel Wilham?' He must approach this with an analytical eye. He had his book to consider.

'I am Sir Lionel's ancestor by marriage. My late husband was Sir Egbert Wilham. I lived at Chinkton Manor all my married life. You two, gifted people possess psychic powers, and that is why you can see me and the reason I have come to see you.'

Sophie stared, awestruck.

'If you need proof of my identity, you will find it in St James' churchyard. My box, as you might call it, Freddie, is close to the white lilac bush, near the vestry.'

'That's where you're buried?' asked Sophie.

'Yes, in the family tomb. I was born in 1732 and died in

1782. Being susceptible to the cold, it was cold that got me in the end. And now,' she continued, 'you wish to know how I appear before you?'

They nodded.

'I draw energy from inner light. This light fluctuates according to how I am feeling. It is this light that enables you to see me in human form. When it fades, I fade, and when my light goes out, I disappear. That is when I rest. Simple really. And now,' she said, abruptly changing the subject, 'how would you both like to go to Lake Windermere?'

four

Adelina glanced through the square leaded windows in the hall, to the garden beyond. At last things were beginning to go her way. She felt warmer and had managed to make friends with two mortals. If events went according to plan, she would soon be re-united with Egbert. But there must be no more accidents. Time was of the essence. Thomas must teach her to glide and soon – securing her place at the manor. If all else failed, she could at least pay regular visits to her husband in the north of England.

She entered the large oak panelled library. The glow from the wood fire lent a soft warm light to the room. And there he was, waiting for her. Thomas bowed, glided to her side, kissed her cheeks and lips. 'I must apologize for not meeting you sooner,' he murmured, stroking her hair. 'But since seeing you last month, I have been inundated with work. Things usually pick up in November.'

'Indeed? That is good to hear.'

He glanced nervously towards the library window.

'Is something wrong, Thomas?'

'I think,' he said fretfully, 'there might be a prospective

client waiting outside. Perhaps she has lost her way. Some do, when they first pass over.' He moved about the room, restless, picking up the odd ashtray, straightening cushions.

'I took your advice,' said Adelina, trying to suppress a feeling of being overlooked. 'And I must say that I do feel a good deal warmer.'

'Good. That is good. Who did you choose?'

'The Reverend George Pym.'

'Yes, a wise choice. Men of the cloth often feel out in the cold, lonely. Their congregation confide in *them* but who do *they* confide in? You used up all your scents, did you?'

'Not all. First I used the apples at the rectory and then the roses outside the church. I have one left: the eau de Cologne.'

'Then make that your reserve. You may need it one day. Has the rector stopped his snoring?'

Adelina nodded. 'Each night I produce the scent of damask roses and he falls to sleep like a baby.'

'And his wife has returned to their bed chamber?'

'Yes. She cannot detect the scents, of course: I tested her out with the apples. Naturally she found her husband's change of behaviour puzzling at first, but now she's so relieved to have him cheerful and loving, she has ceased to worry.'

He gave a small cough. 'And what of Egbert? Any news on that front?'

'I had the good fortune to meet a young man by the name of Freddie Pearson. He is the new butler at the manor.'

'The blond, young man? Yes, I know.'

'After I had visited the rectory and exuded my apple scent, I followed the rector to St James' church. I wanted to ensure that he was gaining some benefit from the smell. I was already feeling warmer, you see, so it appeared that everything was going according to plan. I waited for him in the churchyard, for I wanted to use my second scent, the damask roses, which I did most successfully. It was there that I met Freddie. I knew immediately that he possessed second sight, because I was visible to him and others were not. Later I met Freddie's girlfriend, Sophie, who is also psychic.'

'And where did you meet her?'

'Alongside the wash basins in the ladies' convenience at The Pizza Parlour.'

'The ladies' convenience?'

'I knew that would be the one place I could reach her without Freddie getting in the way. I thought that if I could win the girl's support, she would then persuade her friend to take up my cause.'

Thomas looked doubtful.

'To rescue Egbert from the clutches of Harold and Doris, I need the help of human intervention, you know that, Thomas.'

He grunted. It was difficult to generate much interest where Sir Egbert was concerned. He glanced furtively out of the window. Was the phantom still there? Ghosts regularly merged into their surroundings, particularly if they were of a nervous disposition. Shame to lose her – such a pretty, young thing.

'So tell me,' said Thomas with some effort, 'what have you planned?'

'Freddie and Sophie will travel up to Windermere, in the Lake District. Once there, they will release Egbert's spirit from The Black Dog Inn so that he can return to me, at the manor.'

'And when they first arrive?'

'The couple will liaise with the landlords, Doris and Harold, introducing themselves as mediums and expressing an interest in their "resident ghost" and the tours that they organise for the duped public. Having gained their confidence, they will convince the couple of Egbert's unhappiness. Freddie and Sophie will then suggest a séance, at which Egbert, will appear. This will give him a fair chance to state his case.'

'And then?'

'After Doris and Harold have given their consent for him to leave, Freddie and Sophie will be at liberty to release his spirit so that he can return to me.'

'So you believe that a little enlightenment will do the trick do you, Adelina?'

'You do not like the idea?'

'It is not that I do not like the idea, it is whether the idea will work that concerns me.'

'Why on earth should it not?'

'Gifted psychics do possess the power to un-trap spirits and move them on, that is true. But this couple is young and inexperienced. They need to know what they are doing. Also, it seems that Sir Egbert is suffering from depression, and that could hinder his release, especially as the landlords will be reluctant to let him go.'

'I have taken that into account,' said Adelina. Why did he have to make such an issue of everything?

'Ghosts are sensitive to atmospheres and respond accordingly. Discord is a powerful and destructive emotion, Adelina, and in Sir Egbert's case may prove an impossible force to fight against, especially if Harold and Doris object to his going. Any show of hostility on their part is tantamount to locking Sir Egbert in a cell and throwing away the key.'

'And that, Thomas, is precisely why I am holding the séance. Once the landlords see how unhappy my husband is, they will be merciful and agree to his release. There will be no animosity.'

Thomas gave a dry laugh. 'I doubt that. Appealing to people's better nature rarely works when money is at stake. Ghost publicity creates sensationalism – draws the crowds. But there again,' he said, sensing her disappointment, 'it might be worth a try.'

'Everything is negotiable, Thomas.' She had every faith in her plan.

'But do Freddie and Sophie know how to conduct a sitting?' asked Thomas.

Adelina looked at him blankly. 'It was they who suggested it. Sittings, as you call them, were after my time. I am leaving that part of things to them.'

Thomas frowned. 'Then let us hope that under these risky circumstances, nothing goes awry, for such gatherings can go horribly wrong. Be on hand, Adelina, for anything can happen.'

'I will try to keep a distant eye on events. You must remember,' she said, looking pointedly at her feet, 'that I am restricted in my movements.'

But Thomas was no longer listening. He had spotted the young ghost billowing softly against the wisteria. 'I have to go, Adelina,' he said hurriedly.

Go? He could not go now! 'But what about my gliding lesson? At our last meeting you promised to teach me The Glide.'

'I am afraid we will have to postpone it. I cannot keep my client waiting any longer.'

'You mean that quivering thing hovering over the hydrangeas?'

'You mean the *Wisteria*.'

'The *Wisteria* then.'

'My dearest, she has waited long enough. When I am able, I will most certainly fit you in.'

'Does she have an appointment, this ghost of yours?'

'No.'

'Then why must I be fitted in? It is she who should be fitted in. You are my friend, my teacher and my lover. Does none of that mean anything to you?' Now choking back the tears.

'Adelina, it does. Of course it does.' He removed a stray wisp of grey hair that had escaped her cap. 'But I really do,' he coaxed, already beginning to fade, 'I really do have to go.'

'Just one lesson, Thomas,' she begged, addressing the misty remains of his wig. But Thomas had disappeared, leaving only the smallest of indentations in his chair.

Tears poured down her face as she made her way out of

the library. Once in the passage, she concentrated on lifting herself high enough to clear the floor and having managed this, steered her way towards the open front door. Her feet had never felt so large, her spirit so heavy. She would find Thomas, confront him, in front of his precious client if needs be.

The door to the garden was open and some letters that had been lying on the hall table blew onto the floor. Lady Wilham, on her way to dinner, picked them up and shut the door.

'Dinner is ready, madam,' said Birdie, on her way to the dining room, a bowl of steaming vegetables in her hands.

'Thank you, I'm coming. Switch the radio on, please. I'd like to listen to the concert. It's Bach, one of the suites.'

Moments later, Adelina heard the music; felt the notes vibrate through the soles of her feet. For the first time ever, she felt like dancing. But steps! Could she remember any steps? There was the *German Allemande*, the *Coranto* and the *Sarabande*, all dances that Thomas had taught her. Then there was the *Gavotte*. That was much too fast – all that jumping about. The *Pavan*? Too slow. Oh, well. Fast, slow, what did it matter? She had a mind to dance, and dance she would.

Adelina lifted her arms high above her head: she was a swallow in full flight, flying away to far off lands, swirling, curving, sweeping and dipping. She pointed her toes this way, she pointed them that. There was no counting, no timing and no reprimands from Thomas. Throwing caution to the wind, she stood tall and straight, then giving a small jump, rose from the floor, hovered a few moments, then mindful of the few remaining pieces of porcelain dotted about the hall, coasted towards the foot of the stairs.

Now she stopped and pondered. How many times had she attempted to glide up this staircase? Attempted and failed. No, this time it would be different. If Thomas would not teach her to glide, she would teach herself. The handrails were there to help if Thomas was not. He could burn in hell for all she cared. Inspired by the music, Adelina lifted herself off the ground and glided very slowly, very cautiously up the winding stairs to the first floor. On reaching the landing, she coasted the length of the minstrel gallery taking good care to watch where she was going. She dare not pause to look at the ancestral pictures hanging on the walls: this uncle, that aunt; this baron, that lieutenant colonel; this reverend, that brigadier. Only when she reached the portrait of Egbert, did she stop. The picture hung outside Lady Wilham's bedroom. This had been their room: Egbert's and hers. Only once had she visited it since returning to the manor. It had been in the middle of the night while Lady Wilham slept. Seeing her lying there so peacefully and afraid that she might intrude into her dreams, Adelina had left. But the temptation to stay: to lie beside her, rise with the dawn chorus, watch the bare tree-tops sway through the large bay window and feel the sharp morning chill against her cheek as she lay blanket warmed, was almost too much to bear.

She lifted the latch, but her hands, feathery and frail, were unable to grasp the round, iron handle, so instead, she attempted to pass through the thick, oak panelled door; her ears straining the while to catch the music that had now grown so faint. She tapped her foot: dum, dum, dum di dum dum. Suddenly her toes cleared the floor and to her amazement found herself floating with uncharacteristic grace through the door and into the bedroom beyond. The room, quiet, held an air of sensual luxury: a heady scent, a cashmere scarf draped across a chair. Adelina cried out when she spotted the dressing table Egbert had given her just before she died: their miniature portraits etched into two glass panels that flanked the table's oval mirror. In the far corner, was a long cased clock and next to it a marble-topped console table and a *Brustolon* styled armchair that Adelina did not recognise, stood resplendent near the window.

Then she saw it. In the corner, on top of a writing bureau, stood her old, silver candlestick. There were plant motifs around the base, and the shaft was shaped like a stem and the cup was a Camelia that gently clasped a tapered candle. She touched it, ran her fingers over the smooth, shiny silver. The sight of it, standing there unchanged, enduring, parcelled many mortal memories as she recaptured the redolence of apples, roses, and eau de Cologne. And she could picture the house where she was born set in acres of rich countryside. She was playing hide and seek with her mother; disappearing behind pillars, squeezing into linen cupboards and under tables. And all the time, the candlestick flashed, dazzled and delighted her. Only one thing was missing. The room needed light, not electric, hard and cold but a soft gloaming evensong.

She lifted the candlestick. It was heavy. She held it with both hands and began to dance. Fluted lights, tinsel lights, see the candle – light, bright. Within seconds it had fizzed into life, illuminating the chairs, the bureau, the dressing table and the bed with its abbreviated canopy of gold brocade. On and on she danced. In the ballroom now: Adelina, the best dancer in the county, better even than Lady Drool. Guests admired, praised, applauded. So engrossed was she in all this, so quickly did she turn this way and that, she did not notice sparks flying off in all directions. Within minutes the vesperine glow had changed to one of blinding hostility.

And it was into this that Freddie burst. Through the thickening smoke he could just make out the form of Adelina rotating in the middle of the wooden smoky floor like some over-wound clockwork toy. Now he heard Bea's voice behind him yelling at him to get the fire extinguisher that was at the top of the stairs.

Afterwards, the fire finally out, they flung open the bedroom windows and ran onto the landing, Bea, leaning heavily against the banisters. 'Thank God that the curtains are made of natural fibre, or we'd be coping with toxic fumes as well as everything else. I can't imagine how this started. Will it re-ignite do you think?'

'It shouldn't do. I'll keep an eye on things for a while, just in case.'

He shot back into the bedroom to check on Adelina, but she had gone.

'Freddie, thank you,' said Bea, following him inside. 'You coped admirably.' She pointed to the candlestick now lying on its side in the middle of the room. 'Did you put that there?'

'No, madam.'

Her ladyship sounded at the end of her tether. Since coming to work at the manor, Freddie had heard all sorts of stories about the china going splat and rumours of ghostly goings on. But he felt a certain loyalty toward Adelina, especially with the weekend at Windermere about to happen or not, as the case may be. His first weekend alone with Sophie – boy, was he looking forward to having her to himself. And if Adelina wanted their help – well, who was he to refuse? This was his first real challenge with the spirit world, and with Sophie's support – yes, he would consider it a privilege to work for 'the other side.'

'I know I didn't put that candlestick there,' puzzled Bea, picking it up, and examining it. 'I was in my bedroom just before dinner. That's no more than an hour ago. There's only you and Birdie in the house at the moment, and she, as far as I know, had no cause to come into my room. So who on earth?'

'Oh, my dear lord!' wheezed Birdie, fat and breathless, after mounting the stairs. 'What's happened? You can smell the smoke all over. Are you all right, madam?' She walked into the bedroom, handkerchief over her mouth, gasping and clucking in turn.

'Did you witness anything strange, anything untoward earlier on?' asked Bea, following her.

'Strange? Untoward? No, madam. I was serving your dinner downstairs.'

'The candlestick lying on the floor by my bed; did you put it there?'

'Of course not. Why would I do that?' A peeved note. 'I

don't recall that being on the floor.' Her eyes widened. 'You don't suppose ...'

'I don't know.' Then turning to Freddie, 'You've no doubt heard about our perpetrator?'

'Yes,' he replied, steadily.

'When are you going to Windermere, Freddie?'

'The weekend after next.'

'Spending your lottery money then?' Birdie could see no reason why her ladyship shouldn't know about his small windfall.

'It wasn't much,' he defended, 'but it'll be a help towards the holiday.' He supposed that his four numbers lottery win was Adelina's doing, providing him and Sophie with enough money to cover their expenses.

'I only ask,' said Bea, 'so that I can get things sorted out. After we've cleared this mess up, I shall have to put my thinking cap on.'

'Thinking cap?' Freddie felt a stab of alarm.

'Yes. These so-called accidents have gone far enough. This house is jinxed. I am going to see that it is UN-jinxed.'

five

'Sybil, it's me, Beatrice. Hope I'm not phoning at a bad time.'

'Of course you're not. Haven't heard from you in ages. Isn't that errant husband of yours back yet?'

Bea laughed. It was good to talk to her old school friend, Sybil was such fun – so re-assuring. 'Lionel will be home when he's good and ready. But I'm quite all right on my own, really. Well, almost.'

'You sound a bit down. What's up?'

'I need a ghost tracker. Can you do?'

'A ghost tracker? Let me think. Yes, I've got several on my

books.' There was a pause and then, 'It's the manor again, is it?'

'Yes. There was a fire the other night.'

'Oh, darling! Was anyone hurt?'

'No. It was a relatively small fire and my butler put it out. Sybil, I think it's poltergeist activity again.'

'Look, hang on a sec. and I'll scan my files. Let me see if I can find someone in your area. Most ghost trackers on my books are London based, I'm afraid but – no, here we are. The man arrived in my office this morning and I signed him on. Don't know what he's like, but you can try him.'

'Yes, thanks. I'd ask our rector to perform an exorcism, but I'm not sure that he knows how and I really don't want to involve the church in all this. You know, village gossip and the such.'

'I'll just read out what I've got written here.'

'Please.'

'Colin Drift. Retired computer engineer. Has spent the last five years researching psychic phenomena. To date, he has successfully rid forty houses of unwanted spirits. The equipment he uses is, on his own admittance, unsophisticated. It comprises: a pendulum, tape recorder, a camera and a lot of patience.'

Bea laughed. 'We certainly need plenty of that round here.'

'Colin believes,' continued Sybil, 'that ghosts are nothing more than replays of past events. Thus if a phantom was in the habit of doing such and such when he was alive, he repeats the same action over and over after he has passed over.'

Bea shuddered. 'How simply dreadful.'

'Tedious, certainly. According to Colin, what we actually see are recordings of that activity: rather like watching a video over and over, I suppose. He says that one may witness some pretty hair raising stuff: a re-enactment of a murder for instance, or some other tragedy. A more commonplace occurrence might be the unexplained breakage of an ornament, a door opening or shutting, a picture falling off the wall and so on. Once ghosts know that they are being monitored, they usually, although not always, desist and leave the premises, presumably rest in peace, I don't know.'

Bea sighed, 'Adelina must have been a living disaster in her day. Poor soul. I feel quite bad, shoving her out. Not,' she added without conviction, 'that I really believe in ghosts.'

'Look darling. It's poor you not her, and don't you forget it. All this carry on is enough to send you crackers.'

'Do you think Lionel will mind?'

'Cut out the sentiment, Bea. You're a practical woman, for heaven's sake.'

'You're right. I am.'

'Look, I'll get in touch with this chap now and let you know the results. And Bea?'

'Yes?'

'We must meet soon. Come up to town next month for some lunch and we'll take in a show, it'll cheer you up a bit. Lionel's very naughty, leaving you alone like this. When you write, give him a good telling off from me. We girls must stick together.'

Bea laughed. 'Bye Sybil, and thanks.'

ø ø

'Dear Lionel,' wrote Bea. 'November already. My first November without you! I am writing this in the morning room with Brill and Tope at my feet. Freddie is settling down well in his new job – although the poor boy isn't doing much butlering, apart from answering the door and seeing to my post. But he is an enormous asset around the place doing all the odd jobs I'd normally leave to you! He was wonderful coping with that wretched fire. More on that later.

You may remember that in my last letter I told you that I had contacted Sybil, my old school friend, who runs a psychic agency in London. Well, she has sent me this awful little fellow, Colin Drift, who talks non-stop. I thought he was worth a try – we have nothing to lose, have we? But of course we have, I hear you say – we will lose our family ghost. No answer to that I'm afraid, my darling.

On a more positive note, Colin now assures me that he has done his job, rid the manor of its poltergeist, ghost or whatever it, she, may be, and is leaving this afternoon. He has spent the last few days wandering around the house armed with a pendulum, an ancient looking camera and a portable tape recorder that looks as if it's come out of the ark. He reported some scratchy noises in the attic but they turned out to be mice! But he has sensed a presence in the library, on the stairs, in the drawing room, and most impressively, our bedroom. When I asked him what he did with all this, 'sensing,' he said that he spoke firmly to the entity and asked it to leave. Whether that means it has actually gone, or is just behaving itself for the moment, I don't know, but so far all is calm. Time will tell, I daresay. Anyway, I expect old Sybil will be sending me a hefty invoice any minute! The whole thing is not as satisfactory as I would have hoped, but it was worth a try.

Hope you are not too cross, darling! Look after yourself, my love. Bea.'

Six

When Adelina had glimpsed Freddie it was like a miracle. He would save the manor. He would not let her down. Round and round she whirled. Whiz! passed Freddie. Whiz! passed Lady Wilham. There were flames, there was smoke: thick clouds of it. She heard their screams, their shouts, their orders. Exhausted and terrified, Adelina had dropped the candlestick and like a bullet from a cannon was propelled through the air, away from the manor and onto the village green.

For some minutes she sat on the sodden grass, dazed and shaken. The black beeches, the oaks, the willows, whispered their displeasure. She had started the fire and could not return to the manor, not now. This was the end, the final straw. But what about Egbert? She could not abandon Egbert, not after all this time. If the manor were out of bounds, then she must seek refuge elsewhere. Her plans for his release must go ahead. Nothing should prevent that.

Towards the back of the green where the trees were thickly spread, was a large, weeping willow. Adelina lay down under its dripping canopy, covered herself with a blanket of leaves and put out her light.

Simon was on his way to see George. He always planned to be punctual but he seemed unable to leave his house without something or other delaying him. Last week the washing machine had flooded the kitchen, causing the new vinyl flooring to lift. Yesterday, before leaving for a parochial church council meeting, he had been delayed by a phone call from the organist, who bored him senseless on the merits of the man's recently ordained son. But this morning he had finally cracked it: all his home appliances were in working order and his telephone calls dealt with.

To help him relax, Simon whistled his favourite hymn, 'God Moves in a Mysterious Way.' Unlike prayers, you could conveniently sing hymns on the hoof. Today though, the weather was blustery and his alto voice carried away on the wind.

He headed down Blackbird's Hill, over the green and passed Liz Graham's cottage. Her sitting room light was on. Good. That meant she hadn't left for London yet. On his way home he'd pop round, deliver a church magazine and ask her out. There was a reportedly good production of The Merchant of Venice at The Biddlington Theatre. He would take her to that. Simon was smitten. Liz was his heroine, his life-saver. He still shuddered to think what fate might have dished up had she not radioed him from the air.

The ground was slippery after a heavy downpour and he side-stepped the puddles. He must keep his shoes clean. George had told him off for wearing dirty shoes, and for carrying his vestments in a carrier bag. He expected his curate to dress smartly and quite right too. Simon liked to foster the idea of his boss acting *in loco parentis* and even after all these years remained puzzled as to why his own father had run off with a piano teacher, when Simon was ten. He had missed his dad.

Arriving at the rectory, and while waiting for George to answer the door, he wondered briefly what had been troubling his new boss. When he had first come to Chinkton Green, there had been some talk that the rector was suffering from depression. It was Mrs Herbert, who kept the village stores who had told him: he was liked and respected but the parishioners found him a bit moody. And they would like to see more of his wife, like her to take a more active role in things. Now though, the locals were seeing a change. The rector and his wife were happier and more of a 'couple.' Mrs Pym had even volunteered to hold the summer fete in the rectory garden instead of at the manor, like it normally was.

George opened the front door with a flurry. He was sporting a pair of trendy jeans and a long sleeved sweatshirt with the word, 'Smile,' emblazoned across the chest. 'Hope you like it,' he laughed, seeing Simon's look of dismay. 'Come into the study. Coffee?'

'Thanks. Where did you get the shirt?'

He chuckled. 'I thought of ordering a batch from a marketing manager I know. He gave me this one. Thought they might sell rather well at our summer fete, don't you think?' He walked to the door. 'Sheila,' he called. 'Be a love and bring us some coffee.'

Simon relaxed. 'An excellent idea, George.'

'I thought perhaps a picture of St James printed on the front? Or a slogan like ...'

'*God moves in a mysterious way*?' Strange how poignant those words were.

'Ah yes, Cowper. A fine poet: wrote some of our best known hymns. Now, down to business.' George leaned forward in his seat. 'How do you feel about looking after the parish for one week while Sheila and I go away for a bit of a break? Think you could manage?'

Was this George's way of imbuing him with confidence? Simon wondered. Or was there some vague chance that his rector had a smattering of faith in him after all?

'You've been here long enough to know the ropes,' continued George, 'and Sheila really could do with a rest. So could I for that matter.'

'Well, yes. I think I can cope?'

George shot Simon a questioning look.

'Know. I know I could cope, George.'

'Good. I'm glad to hear it. We plan to go up to the Lake District. To Windermere for one week, starting next Monday. We're staying at her sister's place while they fly off to Nice. A bit of a busman's holiday for us, I'm afraid, but we poor clergymen must be content with the crumbs from the rich man's table.' He laughed merrily, as though he didn't mind the idea of crumbs one bit.

'I'd be pleased to look after things George, and thanks for the show of confidence.'

'I don't believe there's anything too demanding next week.' He thought for a moment before reaching for his diary. 'You've got your hospital visiting list?'

Simon nodded.

'The one important item on the agenda,' said George, flicking through the pages of his diary, 'is a burial of ashes.'

Sheila came in carrying a tray of coffee. 'Morning Simon.'

'Morning Sheila,'

'Drink the coffee while it's hot.' She went out, gently

closing the door behind her.

'Got your diary?' asked George

He nodded.

'We're talking about Thursday, 15th November at 2 p.m. Got that?'

'Yes.'

'It's the ashes of a Mrs Peacock. They are being sent here in advance. By post,' he added, seeing Simon's quizzical expression. 'The parcel will arrive at your house by special delivery the day before the burial: on the Wednesday morning. I've told the deceased's husband, Lawrence Peacock that I shall be away, and for the parcel to be sent to your house: that in my absence you, as curate, will take the service of committal.'

'The Peacocks,' said Simon, thoughtfully stirring his coffee, 'I don't recall a family of that name in the parish.'

'No, they were before your time; left this village some years back. Mrs Peacock loved living here so much she requested that on her death, her ashes be buried in our churchyard. Towards the end of her life the couple moved to Bournemouth in the hope that the sea air might have a restorative effect on her ailing health. Sadly she died last week and was cremated locally, but her ashes, as I said, are being sent back here for burial.'

'I see.'

'Now, you will take the casket or urn, to the burial ground the following day, the Thursday. The service of committal is at two o'clock. Oh, and Simon, will you please give an address, you know, say a few words. It will be expected.'

He nodded and smiled. No worries there. Sermons were his forte.

George helped himself to a sweet digestive biscuit. 'Peacock was a respected member of this community. He donated a large sum of money towards the restoration of the church roof, deathwatch beetle. Quite dreadful that was, the beetle disease, I mean. We had to raise an enormous amount of money to get rid of the pest, and Lawrence was more than generous. That will need a definite mention. He was quite a dignitary in his day too: chairman of the district council and so forth.'

'Why can't this Mr Peacock bring his wife's ashes with him when he comes?' asked Simon draining his coffee cup.

'I think he wants her to stay here overnight. Strange sentiments some people have when their loved ones die. It will be her last stop over, on this earth at any rate.'

'So, who do you reckon will be at the service?'

'Close friends and relatives; about forty or so people, I should think. I'll give you some notes before I leave, so that you can incorporate them into your address.' He smiled encouragingly. 'I'm sure you'll be fine.'

'That sounds straight forward enough,' said Simon glancing at his filofax and admiring his new organisational skills. He'd written all his church commitments in red; a green pen to remind him of people to visit and a blue pen for his personal activities: a flying lesson, he'd decided on a refresher course; a dental appointment – a couple of fillings needed there; and he hoped later to add Liz to his social calendar. Looking at the week of the 15th, he would probably have to plump for the Wednesday: there was the Bible study group Monday, Mother's Union, Tuesday and a television quiz, Saturday. Apart from the Sunday services – he was really looking forward to taking those – he could catch up on a bit of visiting. No, there was nothing too challenging, he supposed.

'That's all settled then,' said George, closing his diary. 'I'm glad that you feel ready to take on the responsibilities of this parish. He looked at him levelly. 'I'm relying on you, Simon. Please make sure you are not late for appointments.'

'Most certainly. And thank you. I appreciate this.'

'Charles Neville is the one to ask if there are any problems. As churchwarden, he knows everything that goes on – more than I do, I expect,' he added dryly.

'Have you the magazines ready for distribution?' asked Simon, eager to catch Liz before she left. 'I um, thought I would pop one in to Liz Graham.'

'Liz Graham? Now there is one parishioner who's slipped through my net. Who is she?'

Simon flushed. 'Liz moved into one of the cottages on the green a couple of months ago. I just happened to bump into her in the village. She's a weekender, she works in town during the week.'

'You seem to know quite a lot about her,' said George, a hint of mischief in his voice.

Sheila caught up with Simon on his way out and thrust a paper bag into his hands. 'A dozen eggs for you,' she said. 'We've far too many for the two of us; thought you might like some.'

'Thanks Sheila. You're looking well,' he added, noticing that she'd also slipped a fruitcake into the bag.

'I am, thanks. Off to Keep Fit now. Must fly. '

'Yes,' said George, watching her climb into her car, 'Sheila's fairly bouncing along these days. It's good to see her looking happy.' He smiled, and his eyes misted. Perhaps, thought Simon, when we know each other better, he'll confide in me as a friend.

Relieved that the meeting had gone so well, he left the rectory feeling he had caught some of their *joie de vivre*. He had never known them so friendly and they were positively bursting with energy. But the best bit of all was George's willingness to leave the parish in Simon's hands.

As he approached Liz's cottage, magazine at the ready, he saw her next door neighbour standing behind his garden gate looking anxiously about him.

'Good morning to you!' called Simon, drawing level with an immaculately manicured privet. 'I'm Simon Guest, the new curate. I don't believe we've met.'

'She's gone,' he said, ignoring Simon's outstretched hand. 'I'm sorry?'

'Pushka, my cat.'

'Oh, dear.'

'Disappeared half an hour ago.'

'What sort of cat is it?' Simon referred to all cats as 'it.'

'A blue, longhaired Persian. She never leaves the garden without me.' He gazed numbly into the distance, his long, grey ponytail whipping round his long pale face.

'I'm sure your cat won't have gone far.' And then in the ensuing silence, 'I'll leave you one of these, shall I?' Handing him a copy of the November issue.

'Hello Simon.' Liz called, walking up to the gate. 'Still no sign of Pushka, Gerald?'

'He shook his head.'

'Come in for a coffee, and a warm. You look all in.'

'No, I must go round the green again. She may have got stuck up a tree. You go inside. I'll be all right.'

'Okay, if you're sure. But I'll be out later.' She turned to Simon. 'Coming in for a coffee?'

'Just for a minute,' said Simon, delighted at this turn of events. 'Not for coffee though. I must do some visiting.' He nodded a quick farewell to Gerald, thankful to be with Liz.

A pile of leaves scrolled across her sitting room carpet as she put her shoulder to the front door and pushed it shut. 'Phew! That's some gale out there. Take a seat.'

'Thanks. But I won't stop. I've brought you a church magazine – thought you might like a read; that's if you've got the time, which I'm sure you haven't.'

'Done anymore flying recently?'

He pulled a face. 'I'm taking more lessons. You know, I thought it was men who were supposed to rescue damsels in distress not the other way round.'

Liz smiled wryly. 'Not anymore.'

He laughed. 'I was wondering. Well, I don't suppose you'd fancy seeing *The Merchant of Venice* at the Biddling-ton Theatre.'

'It's ages since I saw any Shakespeare. Yes, I'd like that.'

'Unfortunately,' said Simon, mentally crossing his fingers, 'it'll have to be on Wednesday week. That is, I'm sorry I can't make the weekend, I'm expected to attend a quiz at the village hall.'

'That's fine. I've a week's leave coming up.'

'Great! Then I'll pick you up at say seven o'clock on the 14th?'

'Lovely, look forward to it.'

'This seems to be the only place affected,' Liz shouted as she opened the front door and was forced back by the gale. 'I switched on the radio earlier and it's calm in the rest of the Midlands. We seem to be the only area getting this foul weather. Poor old Gerald's in a right lather over that cat of his. I must go and help him look for her.' She raised her eyes to heaven. 'She's his life.'

When Simon had gone, she put on her overcoat and went outside.

'You haven't found her then?' she called, seeing Gerald wandering despondently towards his cottage. He shook his head. Oh Lord! thought Liz. I hope she turns up, or I'll never hear the last of it.

Ø Ø

The first thing Simon saw when he opened his front door, was a cat. It was sitting in his hall licking its front paws.

'What the devil –?'

'Mieow!' said the cat.

Muttering to himself, Simon checked the back door and examined the windows. They were all locked. He poured milk into a saucer. The cat lapped it up with its long, pink tongue. Pushka? It certainly answered to the description: long, smoky blue fur and a bushy tail. But how on earth had it got in? And if it were Pushka, what should he tell Gerald? Say he'd found his cat in the lane? Yes, that would do – no harm in stretching the truth a little. But first things first, he must phone the theatre box office and book two tickets for the play. Sifting through the telephone directory, he found The Biddlington Theatre Company, but then realised he hadn't a pencil to jot down the number. The cat began to cry. Simon had never heard a cat cry before. But where was that pencil? He had it only yesterday to do *The Times* crossword. The cat cried louder. 'Shut up you stupid

animal.' All right, so where was the biro? There was a red
biro somewhere. The cat was wailing now. 'You're going
mate, as soon as I've phoned the …' He looked up and
stifled a scream. There, in his armchair, with the cat on her
lap, sat a woman crying very hard and very loud.

With shaking hands, Simon fumbled in his pocket for a
handkerchief and came up with a couple of crumpled
tissues. 'Here, have these.'

'Thank you,' she sniffed, but didn't take them.

'Would you like to tell me what's wrong?' He was burn-
ing to know how she'd got in.

'I was forced to leave my home.'

'Has your husband thrown you out?'

She shook her head. 'But Pushka wants me.'

'You know this cat?'

'We arrived together.'

'Together?'

'I met her on my way here.'

Pushka purred.

'You do realise,' said Simon, unsteadily, 'that this is not
my cat.'

'Of course.'

'And that I must return it to its owner at once.'

'But she is happy with me.'

Pushka purred louder.

'Have you been to social services?'

'I do not understand.'

'About your eviction.'

She stared at him blankly.

Oh, dear. He wasn't dealing with this at all well. 'Coffee?
Would you like a cup of coffee?'

'I never drink, thank you.' She stood up and he noticed
her feet poking out from under a very strange looking
dress. He had never seen such long toes. Perhaps it was
the style of shoe. Very quaint. And there was something
vaguely familiar about her too.

'Is it your son, or your daughter who have thrown you
out?' he asked.

'Neither.' She paused and then, 'I have problems with my feet.'

'Not walking too well?'

'I was trying so hard, you see, and then the fire started and I was forced to leave. And since then, I dare not return.'

'Why not?'

'Because I started it.'

His brain did a somersault. Why hadn't George briefed him about this crazy parishioner? He swallowed hard. Must keep calm. This was all part of his job – part of his ministry.

'Of course,' she went on, idly stroking the cat, 'it was unwise to dance carrying a lighted candle, I see that now.'

'You were dancing with a lighted candle?' My God! The woman was nuts.

'It was wonderful at first. I danced and danced but then as usual things started to go wrong.' Her mouth trembled, 'The curtains caught alight.'

'And the fire? What happened to the fire?'

'It was extinguished. Thankfully. Chinkton Manor is safe.'

Simon froze. His legs gave way and he sank onto the nearest chair.

She smiled. 'Yes, my dear. You remember me now, do you not? I knew the instant I saw you, that very first Sunday when you visited the manor, that you possessed that most blessed of gifts – the gift of second sight. You are a most fortunate young man. We ghosts only make friends with mortals who possess insight and vision. So it is to you that I now turn for shelter.'

Simon stifled a cry.

'Do not be alarmed. It is only for the time being, only until it is safe for me to return to the manor. I will be no trouble, I promise you, no burden on you financially.'

'Oh, no. No, I won't, simply won't believe this. Yes, I admit that I saw someone who looked like you sitting on that rocking chair at the manor, but it was my imagination, had, has now to be my imagination: an hallucination brought on by stress.' He felt his legs weaken and he sat down.

'My name, Simon, is Lady Adelina Wilham, resident ghost of Chinkton Manor.'

He clapped his hands over his ears. 'I won't listen,' he shouted.

'Had my friend,' she continued, tight lipped, 'my once true friend given me the required gliding lessons, the fire would not have started and I would not be sitting here now. But one day I shall master my gliding skills and return to my home. I must return, you see, to welcome my husband.' She glanced around the small, square sitting room. 'It is not the ideal place for me here, of course. 'I am used to having space, plenty of it, but it will have to do for the present.' Her cheeks dimpled. 'You and I have things in common and that is always a good starting point.'

'Things in common? I doubt it.'

'We are both clumsy. Like me, you break things. You are sloppy and unpunctual.'

'I see. Well, thank you very much. Anything else?'

'You can be charming and you are quite nice looking.'

'Right. Well, now that you've got that off your chest, I think you'd better go.'

'Go?' she sat up startled. 'But I have only just arrived.'

Simon stood up and walked unsteadily towards the pile of church magazines awaiting delivery. She could not stay here. Perish the thought. By means foul or fair, he would get her out. He looked at the cat now asleep and softly purring on her lap. 'Give me the cat please.'

'No.'

'Give me the cat.'

'No.'

'Right!' He took hold of Pushka's hindquarters and tried to lift her but she clung fast to Adelina's lap, her claws outstretched, her mouth hissing abuse.

'Now listen, I have to return this cat to its rightful owner, now. Do you understand?' He nursed a scratched wrist.

'Please. Puska likes it here with me. She will be company for me while I am here.'

'I don't care if it likes it here with you, or not. The cat does not, I repeat, does not belong to you. It is stealing, do I make myself clear?'

She stared, defiant. He stared back. A battle of nerves commenced. Simon lost. 'Oh, very well,' he sighed, 'you can stay for two nights and two nights only. On condition,' he added, seeing the shadow of a smile cross her lips, 'on condition that you give me that creature now.'

She scowled and bowed her head.

'I take that to mean a yes,' lifting Pushka by the neck. And as an afterthought, 'Please remember not to touch anything while I'm gone.'

His stomach gave a sickening lurch. 'You won't start another fire, will you?'

'Of course not. There are no candles.'

He grunted, picked up the church magazines, walked towards the door and stopped. 'Do I need to make up a bed?'

'No, thank you. This armchair will do well enough. I sometimes wander about in the night.'

Simon left. He had heard enough.

Gerald – keeping vigil behind heavily draped curtains spotted Simon and Pushka as they walked down the lane towards his cottage. He rushed outside and ran towards them, took the cat without a thank you and enveloped her in his arms burying his horse-like face in her hair. 'Where did you find her?'

'Outside my house,' Simon replied on cue.

'Come along my darling, and Daddy will give her some of her special milk.' He lifted her into his arms 'She likes a drop of brandy when she's upset.'

'Oh, I don't think she's upset. Quite the contrary,' said Simon, unable to resist the dig.

'Thank you for bringing her home.' And with that Gerald

returned to his cottage and slammed the door.

seven

At eight o'clock the following Wednesday, Mrs Peacock arrived by special delivery. A courier, clad from head to foot in squeaky black leather, handed the brown parcel to Simon. Across the front of the square package were the words, 'Urgent,' in red ink. Underneath and in smaller lettering, 'Handle with care.'

Simon laid the parcel respectfully on the hall table. Above him came a series of dull thuds. He ran upstairs and found Adelina in his study, lying flat on her back surrounded by six volumes of his new red leather bound encyclopaedias. This was the last straw! She would go today – pronto! Even with his over developed conscience he had had enough. She was forever careering into things and breaking them. Her creepy wanderings in the middle of the night spooked him so that he had hardly slept a wink.

Then there was the cat: 'her cat', as she called it. Simon had lost count of the number of times he had taken that animal back to Gerald's house. The man hardly spoke to him now, not that he had been any too chatty before. Life was grim and depressing at a time when Simon's energies should have been pouring into his work. This golden opportunity to prove himself in George's absence was eroded daily by forces that were beyond his control. Adelina was perverse, stubborn, irresponsible and ungrateful. When she was not creating havoc, or mooching over Push-ka, she would sit in some kind of trance, her eyes shut, lips moving: communing with her husband, so she said. The whole thing would be ludicrous if it were not so worrying. What if the creature were a figment of his imagination?

What if he were suffering from hallucinations? The idea would not leave him – snaked its way into his mind and lodged there. The thought that he was losing his grip on life scared the living daylights out of him. For nine hellish days – six more than he'd bargained for, he had felt increasingly deranged. What was fact and what was fiction? Fantasy and reality merged unhappily together. He wasted time brooding when he should have been out visiting parishioners; he looked around corners waiting for Adelina to spring out at him and was growing increasingly absent-minded, forgetting to greet people in the village street. The only bright spot on the horizon was tonight's theatre outing with Liz. If only there was someone he could talk to. But who? You had to be careful in a small parish, people gossiped at the drop of a hat, and his reputation as a poor time-keeper was already established; he did not want to offer more bait; Charles Neville would be the first to trot round to the bishop and lodge a complaint, that was for sure.

Simon picked up the volumes and placed them on his desk, while Pushka sat contemptuous and arrogant, indolently licking her paws in the far corner of the room.

'I am sorry Simon,' said Adelina. 'It was clumsy of me, but this house is far too small for me.'

'I think we should have a talk.'

'What about?'

'About your leaving. Today.'

'Today?'

'Yes.'

Her eyes pleaded. 'But where shall I go? And what about my cat?'

'For the last time, it is not your cat. Why do you encourage it?'

Pushka slunk across the room and jumped onto her lap.

'I hoped I could count on your asylum, Simon. These are difficult times and there are more ahead. This weekend, Freddie and Sophie go to Windermere. I need to feel settled so that I may tune into their frequency.'

God! She was still banging on about how she had roped that Pearson lad and his girlfriend into rescuing her husband, or some far-fetched scheme. Simon smiled grimly. Perhaps all this was just an extension of his psychotic state. No, he must not think like that. He was normal, as normal as the next guy and to prove it, he would go and see Freddie today at the manor and talk this whole business through. Trouble was, he didn't know the fellow that well. Could he trust him to keep quiet? Look! He was at his wit's end, wasn't he? Right. Then he would risk it.

By this time Adelina had managed to get to her feet and was sitting in his swivel chair sifting through some papers lying on his desk. 'Is that Mrs Peacock on your hall table?' she asked casually.

He started. 'The remains of her, yes. How did you know?'

She shrugged.

'Silly question. Of course, you know everything, don't you?'

Adelina stuck out her chin. 'I will not leave.'

'You will, please.' Trying to steady his legs as he walked to the door, 'I am popping round to the manor to see Freddie Pearson and I would like you gone by my return.'

'But –'

'No buts, Adelina. I am sorry to sound harsh, but that is the way it is. Now, before I go, are there any messages you would like me to give him?'

'Freddie? Oh yes,' her tone was plaintive. 'He and Sophie know what to do. But tell him that I will keep an eye on the proceedings. Although how I shall manage do so, living in limbo, I do not know.'

'That's it, is it?'

A small nod, a tremble of the mouth.

Eager to be gone, he hated to see anyone cry, Simon hurried out of the room, down the stairs and through the front door.

Ø Ø

Simon marched up the manor steps and pressed the door bell. Freddie opened the front door, his sleeves rolled up to the elbow.

'Might I have a word, Freddie?' He felt faint, nauseous. 'I would have called at your home – hate disturbing you at work, but it is pressing.'

'You all right Mr Guest?'

'A bit dizzy.' He swallowed. 'It'll pass in a moment.' But he felt himself sway.

'You'd better come in and sit down Mr Guest.'

Simon hesitated. The last thing he wanted was to bump into Bea. 'Lady Wilham's out shopping, by the way,' said Freddie, as though reading his thoughts. A couple of minutes later Freddie returned from the kitchen with a glass of iced water that Simon drank thirstily.

'I wonder what brought that on?' Taking his empty glass, he led the way round the side of the house, down some terrace steps, towards an old *Cedar of Lebanon*. 'I come here for a smoke,' now taking out of his pocket a crumpled packet of cigarettes. 'It's quiet – we're not likely to be disturbed here.'

Simon sat against the bole of the tree. From here he could see the maze with its little box-like compartments. 'I don't know where to begin.'

Freddie blew smoke rings into the morning air. 'Try the beginning.'

'Does the name Adelina mean anything to you?'

'What?'

'Adelina. Do you know the name?'

'Yeh, I heard you the first time.'

'Well?'

Silence. Then, 'Yes, I know her.'

This was better than absolution, thought Simon. 'I'm not going mad then?'

'Not unless I am too.' Freddie frowned. 'Tell me more.'

'She's camping in my house.'

'What! You mean she's actually haunting your pad?'

Simon nodded. 'A bit of a come down from the manor, isn't it?'

'We wondered you see, Sophie and me, where she'd gone after the fire and all that. She just vanished – left no clues: nothing. She wants us to be her envoys, you know.' He paused. 'I don't suppose you know about all that do you?'

'The trip up north? Oh yes, she told me. I didn't believe her though. I mean, it's all so bizarre, isn't it?'

Freddie's eyes narrowed. 'It makes sense her coming to you, a clergyman – sensitive, mystical, all that stuff. Yeh, I can see why she's chosen your place. Anyway, it's good to know she's okay.'

'Yes, well she might be, but I'm not. The creature's driving me round the twist.'

'Adelina's not the easiest of creatures, I grant you.' Freddie stubbed out his cigarette, placing the butt end into his apron pocket.

'Easy? She is stubborn, clumsy and creepy. The creature pokes about in my cupboards, knocks things over and causes total chaos. Do you realise Freddie, that we are being manipulated by, by …'

'By a ghost? Yeh.'

'Well doesn't that bother you the tiniest bit?'

'It did at first. It doesn't anymore though. Not really.'

Simon gave a dry laugh. 'I don't know how you can remain so calm.'

Freddie eyed him sharply. 'Does anyone else know about this?'

'No. And they mustn't,' he added quickly. 'You're not planning on telling anyone are you?'

'Of course not. She has to be protected.'

'*She* has to be protected, what about us? She might do anything – whip us off to the other side or something equally ghastly.' Freddie obviously had no idea of the implications; it was probably just one huge game to him.

'And another thing,' he added heatedly, 'If the bishop gets to hear of this, my sanity will be in question not to mention my job.'

'Calm down, Mr Guest. The manor fire wasn't that big. I know, because I put it out. It obviously gave her a fright – I doubt that she will repeat the exercise.'

'That's not entirely the point,' said Simon, an edge to his voice. 'Why are you so casual about the whole thing?'

'Hardly casual. I take an interest in the supernatural, Mr Guest. Sophie and I regard it as something of a privilege to have been asked to help the other side. We should lend our support – all of us.'

'You think I should let her stay, don't you? That's what you're driving at, isn't it?'

'You're putting the words into my mouth but yes, it would be a kindness. She's obviously too terrified to move anywhere after what happened. Her gliding skills are pretty dire, you know.'

Simon sighed, his conscience all at the ready. 'All right. For how long?'

'For as long as it takes.'

'How long is long?'

'Look,' humoured Freddie, 'with any luck, Sophie and I should be able to release Egbert's spirit by this weekend. If we do, then he'll return to the manor and so will Adelina. That ghost buster chap believes he got rid of her, so she's quite safe from the likes of Lady Wilham, at least for the time being.' He paused. 'Did Adelina say anything by the way – send any message?'

'Yes. She wishes you and Sophie both well and says she will be keeping an eye on the proceedings, whatever that means.'

'Ah, that's good. Thanks. And if we need her advice?'

'She'll be at my place. Do I have to do this Freddie?'

'It's up to you, Mr Guest.'

Simon hesitated. The thought of one more day, one more minute of her presence made him feel sick. But it was good, felt wonderful to know he was not mad that his secret was now shared with another. He gave a deep sigh. 'All right. I relent; you win. She can stay but only until you return from Windermere; after that she is on her own. As things stand, I can't sleep, eat or run a parish. Look at me!' He managed a weak smile. 'I'm a wreck.'

'You're a gem, Mr Guest.'

'That too!'

They laughed, shook hands and parted.

Ø Ø

Simon crept into his house, closed the front door and listened. The silence was too eerie for comfort. He stood in the hall, ears strained, not daring to move. The clock chimed the hour. One minute, two minutes went by, still no sound. Had Adelina gone, really gone? He scanned the hall, everything was in its place; nothing upset, nothing broken. There was his jacket hanging over the banisters, where he had left it and the rug lay squarely in the centre of the wooden floor. A pile of church magazines, neatly stacked, was placed next to the small brass gong on the hall table. And yet something was wrong, very wrong. He could feel it.

His brain did a series of clicks. Parcel! Check the parcel. Panic! Where was the parcel? He had left it on the hall table ready for tomorrow's service. Simon looked on the floor, searched in the kitchen, the sitting room, the bathroom, under the beds, inside the wardrobes but there was no sign of it anywhere. No parcel, no burial, no job!

'Adelina!' he bawled. 'Adelina!' Breathless, he stopped. The cat! Where was the cat? 'Pushka! Pushka!' Nothing. Adelina, Pushka and Mrs Peacock had all gone.

The telephone rang compounding his panic: 'Is that The Reverend Guest?'

'Yes.'

'Peacock here. Just checking that the urn arrived safely.'

Simon took a deep breath. He must at all cost keep calm.

'It did. It did.' That bit was true, at least.

'Splendid. Always a bit of a worry sending by post, especially if it's one's wife.'

What a tasteless joke, thought Simon, who, on the point of answering, began to feel his fears, his frustrations slowly disperse. A curious light headedness descended on him, and he felt as though he were looking down on himself, no longer affected by anything around him.

'You there Mr Guest?'

'Yes, yes.' Sprayed with opiates, perhaps?

'There will be about forty-five of us at the service tomorrow afternoon.'

Mr Peacock sounded a very long way off. Simon closed his eyes.

'Just my wife's friends and relatives, you understand.' A pause: 'You are there, Mr Guest?'

'What? Oh, yes. That's terrific, Mr Peacock – just terrific.'

'Terrific?'

'That's what I said. I say it should be terrific fun!'

'Terrific fun! I would remind you Mr Guest, that my wife has just passed away, not won a two week's cruise to the Bahamas.'

Why was Mr Peacock shouting? Simon was only trying to cheer the man up. Better try again. 'So, you liken your wife's passing to a cruise, do you?'

'What?' he barked.

'A beautiful way to describe her onward passage.'

'Are you out of your mind?'

'And I am sure, that when your wife reaches her destination, the Pearly Gates will be opened wide ready to receive her. You mark my words, Mr Peacock.'

'Oh, I have marked your words, all right Mr Guest, and so will your rector when he returns, be assured of that.'

'But why?' Simon's forehead wrinkled in gentle bemusement. 'I only wish to offer my condolences.'

'This conversation has gone far enough, shouted Mr Peacock. 'I will expect you tomorrow at St James' church –

two o'clock prompt.' He slammed down the phone.

Head drooped; Simon made his way into the kitchen. *'Behind a frowning providence he hides a smiling face,'* prompted the words of the hymn. Perhaps Mr Peacock had a smiling face. He doubted it.

Pouring himself a large glass of sweet sherry, a welcoming gift from the Mother's Union, he sat down, put his feet on the kitchen table and dazedly thought of his theatre date with Liz. This fogged out feeling would not shift. Now it was making him feel tired. Simon closed his eyes and within minutes was asleep. He dreamt that Adelina, Pushka, Gerald and Mr Peacock were all flowing effortlessly through the funnel of a ship and out into space, never to be seen again.

The theatre was full and as Simon glanced round the newly furbished auditorium, with its red plush seats and freshly painted proscenium arch, his problems seemed totally preposterous. How could he have become so stressed about some silly ghost? She had gone, hadn't she? As for the parcel, well, that would no doubt, turn up in the fullness of time. Time – that was something he did not have, a small voice warned. Later, later – he would worry about it later. For now, all he wanted was to sit next to Liz, enjoy her company and watch the play. If only he could shake off this sluggishness, this tiredness, this feeling of being cut off from everything.

'Are you all right, Simon?' Liz asked. They were drinking their gins and tonic during the interval.

'Fine. Absolutely fine.'

'You seem a bit …'

'A bit what?'

'I don't know – a bit absent, distracted.'

'I'm just tired, that's all.' They found a couple of empty seats and drank in silence; the bar was noisy and full.

'How's the parish?' asked Liz wishing conversation was not so thin on the ground. 'Working out all right without the rector?'

'Fine; couldn't be better.'

'Well,' said Liz after a moment's pause, 'you have certainly made one convert.'

'Oh? Who's that?'

'Gerald's cat, Pushka.'

'She's gone again, I'm afraid.'

'Not anymore,' said Liz. 'Pushka padded back to Gerald's earlier today.'

Well, at least Adelina had not stolen it; one problem less, he supposed, as they headed back to the auditorium and sat down. Simon shivered. Strange, the theatre felt quite warm earlier. He noticed that a woman had moved into the empty seat on his left; perhaps she had created a temporary draught. He glanced at Liz who didn't look at all chilly.

'Wonderful acting!' said the newcomer.

'Yes,' agreed Simon, eyes front as the curtain rose.

'What did you say?' Liz.

'Nothing, Liz.'

'I have come to see my son,' said the woman on his left. 'He makes a wonderful Bassanio. Plays just for his mother, you know.'

Simon knew all right – knew that voice. He turned, stifled a scream. 'You!'

'Shush!' said a man sitting behind.

'What's going on?' said Liz.

'I want it back.' Simon said.

'You want what back?' asked the woman.

'The urn. The ashes – Mrs bloody Peacock.'

'Will you kindly leave the theatre, sir,' said a man with a

torch.

'Turn that torch off.' Simon said.

'You are causing a disturbance, sir.'

Simon rapped the empty seat beside him. 'You've got the wrong person, squire. Ask her. She's the one.'

'Out!' said the steward.

'Excuse me Liz,' said Simon.

What's going on?' Liz responded.

'You scheming witch.'

'Simon!'

'Not you, Liz. Her.' Pointing to the empty seat.' Oh, God!'

'Out!' The man with the torch.

'I'm coming.' Stumbling his way to the end of the row.

'Drugs,' someone said, as he stepped over legs.

'Drink,' said another, as he was marched up the aisle.

'A menace,' said a third, sitting in row G.

'Is he violent?' asked the woman at the box office, as Simon was hauled through the foyer, out of the main doors and onto the street.

Outside, it was cold and drizzly, the pavement, sleek with wet. Simon drew up his coat collar, looked up at the theatre and wondered if he could get in through the back, without being seen.

There was a sudden flash of green as Adelina rushed passed him, took a left and disappeared through a door marked, 'Circle and Upper Circle.' 'Hey stop!' yelled Simon, running after her. Up he went, one floor, two floors, taking the steps, two at a time. For a ghost with gliding difficulties, she was surprisingly nifty. He stopped to catch his breath before rounding the third bend where he discovered her sitting with her feet pointing upwards, directing his eye to a photograph of Sir John Gielgud that hung immediately over her head.

'All right, Adelina,' he panted. 'The game is up.' But she scrambled to her feet and made off again. He climbed wearily on until he reached the upper circle. There was no attendant at the door, so he slipped inside, stood at the entrance and scanned the audience. The auditorium was dark, but there was enough light coming from the stage to make out some of the faces. After padding up and down the aisles, he sensed something hovering directly above him. He looked up and saw Adelina sitting cross-legged over his head.

'Why are you giving me the runaround?' he hissed.

'Be quiet. I am watching the play.'

Exhausted, Simon sat on the gangway steps and laid his head in his hands and as Gratiano brought the play to its close, the rapturous applause did nothing to raise his spirits. Even Adelina landing at his side, did little to cheer him. She clapped furiously.

'The parcel, Adelina. Please,' he added lamely.

'Is not Maurice wonderful?' her face alight with adoration. 'See how he bows. What a fine doublet and hose. He is a far better actor than the billed Bassanio, do you not think.'

'If you say so. I am too tired to argue. Look, Mrs Peacock's burial service is tomorrow. If I do not have her ashes in my possession, there will be nothing to bury not to mention an almighty stink. Don't you have any sense of right or wrong?' He groaned. For this to happen on his first date and with Liz of all people, the one person he wanted to please, to thank, to love. Liz! He must get back to Liz!

☿ ☿

'You were wonderful!'

'Thank you, mother.'

'Quite the best Bassanio I have seen. You balanced rhythm with meaning quite beautifully. How I wish the rest of the audience had seen you, had witnessed your performance.'

'Your friend. Could he not see me?'

Adelina shrugged. 'Simon sees what he wants to see. He

is certainly blind to my needs.'

They were sitting in the costume department. It was a large, untidy basement that also housed the theatre boiler. The two of them perched on a large wicker basket brimming over with bulky gowns, petticoats, gloves and hats.

'You look pretty peaky, mother. Is all well?' asked Maurice, glancing suspiciously at the square shaped parcel resting on her knee.

'No, all is not well. The curate has thrown me out. I am a refugee again.' She pouted. 'You do not suppose ...'

'No, mother,' he cautioned, 'you cannot stay here; certainly not. The two of us would cause mayhem, you know that. I am also in danger of eviction, you know.' He sighed with longing. Recognition, that was what he yearned for. But apart from his mother's occasional visits, he doubted very much that anyone ever actually saw his performances. Oh the theatre folk were aware of his presence all right, he made sure of that. But to them he was merely a gremlin. 'Gremlins,' they murmured, when he put an occasional spanner in the theatrical works. On the first night of *The Merchant of Venice*, he had removed Portia's picture from the leaden casket and placed it in the gold. On the second night, the actor playing Shylock had found himself quoting Antonio's lines instead of his own. All hell was let loose. Shylock was sacked and the props lady left in a huff. Maurice felt a bit bad about that.

'What is that you are carrying, mother?' He disliked dwelling on his wayward streaks.

'I wanted to teach him a lesson,' she said.

'You wanted to teach whom a lesson? Please do not be vague; it is late and I am tired.' He could have done without her company tonight – was out of sorts.

'Simon, the curate, of course. He told me to leave his house, ordered me out, because he says that I am clumsy and break things.'

'Which you do.'

'Which I do – I admit I do and that is why Lady Wilham wanted to be rid of me as well, and now you are cross with me.' Tears splashed down her cheeks.

'Ah, Mother, do not start crying, please.' He put his arm around her, tried to suppress a slight feeling of irritation. 'You are far too sensitive. You must learn to organise yourself better. Now tell me truthfully, have you stolen that parcel?'

'Yes.'

'From the curate?'

'Yes.'

'And what is in the parcel?'

'The ashes of a one time parishioner.'

He eyed her sharply. 'You have not been disturbing the graves, have you, mother?'

'Of course not. They were sent to the curate's house for burial tomorrow afternoon.'

'So, why did you take them?'

'I wanted to pay the curate back for telling me, ordering me to go.'

Maurice alighted from the basket. 'Very well. Now you know what it is you must do?'

'Yes, Maurice. I must return them.'

'At once.'

'But I cannot, Maurice. Not after tonight.'

'You can. The curate will be so relieved to have them returned he will let you stay on. Now dry your eyes and off you float.'

'You know perfectly well, that I cannot float,' she snapped. 'It is a miracle I arrived here at all.'

'Where is Thomas? I thought he was helping you with all that?'

'He was,' she pouted. 'But not anymore. He has deserted me. I will just have to manage on my own.'

He took her hand. 'Poor Mother. Tell me, how many scents have you used up?'

'Two. I have one left – the eau de Cologne.'

'Then try that. It might attract his attention.'

'Only as a last resort. I am done with Thomas.'

'You know, Mother,' he said, opening the basket and

sifting through a pile of nightshirts, 'I find everlasting life damned tedious, do you?'

'I do. Absolutely, and lonely.'

'All everlasting life does, is to provide us with endless opportunities to commit follies that we would like to have tried during our lifetime, but never had the nerve. The one advantage of being mortal is that it allows us to bow out gracefully before we make complete fools of ourselves.' He picked a pair of embroidered gloves, decorated with ribbons. 'We must pray for Father's safe deliverance,' he said, slipping his long fingers into them. 'Once he is back home at the manor, I shall visit you both.' He would like to see his father again, although he doubted that things would be any better between them. 'Do you think, Mother,' now trying on a wide brimmed hat trimmed with feathers, 'that he would have approved of my performance tonight?'

'My dear, your father would have been immensely proud.'

'Would he?' Maurice doubted it. So many years ago now, but he could still remember the little theatre tucked away at the back of the manor where he and his young friends had performed in front of their parents and friends. His mother had clapped, cheered and encouraged, but his father always looked bored to tears for some reason. The harder Maurice tried to impress him, the more bored his father became. He would fidget, talk, or rock on his chair. Maurice pulled out all the theatrical stops too: he took the largest parts, spoke the loudest, pulled funny faces, stuck out his little chest and swanked across the stage. But the sillier he became, the more fidgety his father grew. As the years went by, the plays grew fewer then ceased altogether. The little theatre with its chandelier and candles remained in darkness: became dusty and damp with misuse. His father insisted Maurice devote his time to studies and leave acting well alone. But Maurice knew what he wanted. He wanted to become an actor like David Garrick.

His mother took him to see *Othello* and *King Lear* at Drury Lane, while his father regarded all thespians as no better than servants and the stage, a highly unsuitable profession for the future baronet of Chinkton Manor. And so Maurice's thwarted ambition, coupled with a growing resentment for his father was buried deep within him.

He kissed Adelina abruptly on the cheek – the past was best kept under wraps. 'Goodnight, Mother. And thank you for coming.'

'Good bye, Maurice.' She hated farewells, but any sentiment was swamped by an overriding dread of the return journey. How she loathed astral travel, but it was imperative to think positively to convince herself that she could move with grace and efficiency.

Adelina closed her eyes, and imagined that she was travelling on the seam of a cloud: drifting gracefully along a course that would set her down safe and sound in Simon's house. In her effort to concentrate, she quite forgot about the parcel.

nine

Simon rushed down the theatre steps and into the street. It was still raining and as he peered through the drizzle, he saw Liz standing outside the front entrance. He called to her, weaving his way through a group of noisy students. 'I'm so sorry,' he said, arriving breathless at her side. 'So terribly sorry.' She stared stonily ahead. 'Liz, I mean it. I can explain.'

'Can you?'

'I was looking for someone.'

'Really? You chose a funny time to do so, I must say.'

'Yes, well, she's a funny woman.'

'Oh, is she?'

'Look, I can explain.'

'So you've said.'

'Not here, Liz. Let's go home.'

A taxi drew up to the kerb and she climbed in without a word.

'Liz! Speak to me. Send the taxi away. Please!'

'Too late.' This, as she gave the driver instructions.

'Can I come and see you back at the cottage?'

'No. I've had about all the excitement I can stand for one night. It isn't every day I'm asked out by a man who talks to himself during the performance and goes walkabout in the last act.'

She slammed the door and the taxi drove off, leaving Simon staring after her as rain trickled down his nose and into his mouth.

'You still here, sir?' asked the doorman. 'It's getting late. Hadn't you best be getting home?'

'What?' Simon looked down at his jacket – it was soaked. He shivered. What time was it? Everyone seemed to have gone. He glanced at the doorman. He seemed a sensitive guy, perhaps he had seen Adelina. There was no knowing who was psychic these days.

'Excuse me,' he called, as he watched the old man close and lock the theatre doors.

'Yes?'

'You haven't by any remote chance seen a middle aged woman wandering about the theatre, have you? She was wearing a long green dress, and a white mob cap.'

'One of the actors is she?'

Phew! The man didn't think he was mad then. 'Not exactly no – more a …'

'A friend?'

'That's right, a friend.' What a nice, helpful chap!

'I don't usually go backstage mate. Out front is my domain, but I can enquire for you, if you like.' The doorman looked at him narrowly. 'Wasn't you causing a spot o' bother earlier was it?'

'Me? Only concern – for my friend, I assure you.'

'The one you have lost?'

Simon nodded.

'Right. I'll go and ask round the back for you.'

'That's most awfully kind. I'm allowed in am I?'

'I s'pect it's all right.' He shot him an uncertain look before shuffling into the theatre where he walked to a door at the back of the foyer marked, 'Private.'

'A friend you say?' He didn't turn round.

'That's right, a friend.' The sort you need like a hole in the head, Simon muttered under his breath.

'I can but ask.'

'Thank you. Thank you so much.'

'Oh!' he stopped. Her name. I forgot to ask the lady's name.'

'Adelina.'

'Adelina. Right. Be back in a shake.'

Simon sat on a plush seat sandwiched between the box office and the theatre entrance. He hoped the man with the torch didn't show up. The evening had been an utter disaster. Liz would never speak to him again and to lose the remains of a one-time parishioner was unforgivable. The incident would be viewed in a very dim light. The bishop would be consulted, the press alerted and all hell let loose. Even kindly old George wouldn't listen to this one, and revealing the truth might prove even more hazardous than keeping his mouth shut. Nothing made sense anymore. The events kept jumbling around in his head like an unsolved jigsaw puzzle. He still felt dazed but less so, hardly any wonder after all his chasing about. His head felt clearer though and that strange, drugged feeling had finally lifted.

Perhaps he dozed off for a few minutes, or was lost in thought, but the next thing he knew, he was being shaken vigorously by the shoulder.

'Excuse me sir.'

Simon's head shot up. A policeman?

'Police Constable Clark, sir.'

'I don't understand.'

'It seems,' said the Constable 'that nobody has seen your lady friend. However,' he referred to his notebook, 'A Miss Merle O'Leary, in charge of the costume department, found this brown paper parcel while putting away some theatrical clothing. It was discovered near a large wicker basket. This is yours I take it? It has your name on it.' He dangled it under Simon's nose and he went to take it. 'Officer! Thank you so much.'

'Not so fast, Mr Guest,' he said, drawing the parcel close. 'I think we should open this together, at the police station.'

'The police station?' And then, 'Oh, I see – as a safety precaution, you mean. But I can explain. It's quite simple. This parcel contains …'

'Yes?'

'Human remains.'

'Human remains? I see sir. I have a car waiting that will escort us to the station. Shouldn't take too long.'

'But you don't understand, Constable.'

'I don't think I do sir. Yet.'

'I am curate of St James, Chinkton Green. I am not wearing my clerical collar, because I am off duty, but I can assure you that is who I am.' He would like to wring that doorman's neck. And while he was on the subject, where was he? He scanned the foyer but there was no sign of him.

'Can you provide proof that you are curate of Chinkton Green?'

Proof? Had he proof? Think man. He fumbled inside his jacket. The church magazine! That would solve it. 'See?' he screeched, aware of a note of madness entering his voice, as he withdrew a dog-eared, November issue from his pocket. Constable Clark barely glanced at it.

'That is not sufficient proof, I'm afraid. And even if it were, we would still need to examine this parcel thoroughly. What was it doing in the costume department of the Biddlington Theatre? Who is this missing lady? All questions that need verification sir, if you don't mind?'

'Mind? Of course I mind. Look, Constable, I have had a trying day in the extreme. And not to put too fine a point on it, I need that parcel tonight. Do I make myself clear?'

'Very clear sir.'

'Are you arresting me?' Simon's voice pitched to its limit. 'Because if you are, just say so, put the handcuffs on me and be done.'

'Calm down sir. We are not charging you, and you are not obliged to come if you so wish. However, it is in your own interests and it won't take long, so I advise that you follow me now.'

'Officer,' said Simon, lowering his voice, 'tomorrow, I have to bury that parcel.'

'Of course you do. Now are you coming or not?'

Simon nodded lamely.

'Thank you. We appreciate your cooperation.'

He followed Constable Clark to a waiting car where he sat glumly on the back seat watched by a small group of onlookers who had suddenly appeared from nowhere. Once at the Biddlington Police Station, Simon was escorted to an interview room. He sat on a high-backed chair that was placed opposite an old battered desk. A few minutes later, a uniformed policeman walked in, followed by a younger police officer carrying the parcel and a mug of steaming liquid.

'Good evening, sir,' said the policeman, placing his considerable bulk behind the desk. 'My name is Sergeant Black and this is Officer Bostock. Is that my tea, Bostock?' he barked, as he took a tape recorder out of the desk drawer before slamming it shut.

'Yes, sergeant.'

'This it?' A sharp nod at the parcel.

'Yes, sergeant. We can verify that the package contains human ashes, in an hurn.'

'Urn, Bostock – urn.' He clamped cold eyes on Simon. 'Tea?'

'Er, no thank you. As I said before, I am the curate of St James, Chinkton Green and …'

'Disgusting!'

'I'm sorry?'

'The tea – disgusting. When was this made Bostock, yesterday?'

'If,' ventured Simon, 'I might be permitted to telephone the church warden, Mr Neville, he will identify me and the parcel.'

'Hang on, hang on.' Sergeant Black pressed the record button on his cassette player, and logged the necessary details. 'Right,' he said at length, sitting back in his chair. 'You were saying.'

'Yes. If you would just allow me to telephone Mr Neville, he will identify me and the parcel.' Why had he not thought of that at the theatre? Stress, he supposed.

'I see. The parcel being?'

'The ashes of the late Mrs Peacock.'

'Tell me, sir,' said Sergeant Black taking a gulp of his tea, 'Tell me, are you in the habit of taking the ashes of a deceased member of your flock to the theatre of an evening?'

'No, I am not.' What an unpleasant little man.

'Then why, pray, did you take them with you tonight?'

'I didn't.'

'You didn't?'

'No. They were found in the costume department after the performance.'

'I know that,' snarled the sergeant.' But how did they get into the costume department in the first place?'

Simon cleared his throat. 'They must have been left there by someone.'

'That someone being?'

'My friend.'

'The friend you lost?'

'Yes.'

'At the theatre?'

'Yes.'

'I see. So where do you think this friend is now?'

'I don't know, but if I could just phone Mr Neville ...'

'In a moment. Now, what is your relationship with this lady?'

Simon paused. 'Which one?'

'Oh, you have several. Lucky man.' The sergeant shared the joke with Officer Bostock, who smiled weakly. 'The one to whom I allude, the one who was last seen wearing a form of fancy dress.' He referred to some notes. '"A long, green dress and a mob cap." That is your description, sir?'

'Yes.' Simon paused. 'She is just a friend.'

'Very good. So what might an elderly lady such as your friend, be doing walking around with an urn containing the ashes of a Mrs Peacock?'

'I don't know. Maybe she felt attached to them – her.'

'Mrs Peacock?'

'Yes.'

'Did your friend know Mrs Peacock?'

'I don't think so, no.'

'Were you a friend or relative of the deceased, sir?'

'No.'

'Then what is your interest in all this, please?'

'Interest?' Simon's throat throbbed with indignation. 'My interest, as you put it Sergeant, was in finding the ashes in time for tomorrow's burial. It would hardly look good my turning up without them, would it? Especially as I am the clergyman conducting the service.'

'It seems,' said the sergeant, leafing through some notes, 'that we don't have her surname. Being a friend of hers, you would, I take it, know her surname.'

Simon looked blank. If only he had time to think.

'Well?'

'Guest,' he whispered.

'She shares your surname then, does she.'

'Yes. You could say that.'

'Adelina Guest,' Sergeant Black elocuted, prodding his double chin with a pencil. 'That's very interesting. You didn't say she was a relative – a friend is what you said, sir.'

Simon moistened his lips. 'She is a friend as well as

my ...'

'Your what, sir?'

'Aunt. My great aunt.'

'Great Aunt Adelina.'

'That is correct. On my father's side,' Simon added hurriedly.

'I see. So what is her interest in the ashes?'

'My great aunt is eccentric – she likes collecting unusual things.'

'Such as human remains?'

'Well, I wouldn't put it quite like that.'

'No? Then how would you put it?' Sergeant Black slurped more tea.

'Aunt Adelina is lonely. Perhaps she thought they would look well on her mantle piece – keep her sort of company.'

'Mr Guest. If what you tell me is true, and you are protecting this lady, it could make you an accessory. Do you understand what I am saying?'

Simon nodded.

'If she is guilty of stealing the urn, we may have to prosecute.'

'Really,' panicked Simon, 'I don't think there is any need for that.'

'It isn't up to you, sir.' Sergeant Black's face was pale and set. 'It will be up to Mr Peacock. Should he choose to press charges, there would be further inquiries. An arrest may have to be made.' He looked at Simon with distaste before turning to the constable. 'Make a note of Mr Lawrence Peacock's address. It's on the back of the parcel.'

'Yes, Sergeant.'

'Now your aunt's address, please,' he snapped, stepping up the volume.

'Address?'

'Yes, Mr Guest. Where does she live?'

Simon bit his lip.

'Well? Come along, I haven't got all night. Bostock?' he growled, picking up the mug and thrusting it into the constable's hand.

'Yes Sergeant.'

'Don't ever give me that muck again.'

'No Sergeant.'

'Now, one more time, Mr Guest, Where does your aunt live?'

Simon swallowed. 'With me – temporarily, that is.'

'And her fixed address?'

'She has none,' he spluttered. 'As far as I know. Very vague, my aunt. Flits about all over the place – most disconcerting. Takes off on a whim.'

'Takes off where, Mr Guest?'

'Oh, she never tells me – very independent. Quite a goer for someone of her age.' Simon's right leg had started to twitch.

'I hope you are telling the truth, young man. Because if not, you are, in two words: for it. Covering up for anybody – anybody at all is a criminal offence. Do I make myself clear?'

'Yes, Sergeant. And if I hear from her I will be in touch post haste.'

Sergeant Black switched off the recorder and stood up. 'Officer! Check Mr Guest's identity with a Mr Charles Neville of Chinkton Green then providing everything is in order, we can all go home to bed.'

Ø Ø

Simon fumbled for his front door key and let himself in. It was wonderful to be home. For a few moments he listened to that now familiar silence – a silence interrupted only by the hot water pipes giving the odd comforting burp as they settled for the night. He clutched the parcel close to his chest. Where should he put it for safe keeping? Here, in the hall or in the sitting room? No, upstairs might be safer. Under his bed? In it perhaps? He shuddered at the thought; but drastic times called for drastic measures. After climbing the stairs, each felt mountain steep, Simon

opened his bedroom door and still clasping the urn, collapsed fully clothed onto his bed, where he fell into an
exhausted sleep.

ten

It was dark. So black was it, Adelina could only spy tiny
pockets of light from the configuration of stars above. She
smelt yew and when she put out her hand, prickly branches scratched her fingers. She felt trapped, boxed in. But
she dared not move for fear of taking off again and of
finding herself in some worse place. Trembling and afraid,
she sat on the damp earth and waited for day.

Ø Ø

Sir Egbert sat perched on a bar-stool. In a moment he
would move to one of the more comfortable pews over by
the fireplace. Pews were all the rage these days. In his time
they were meant for churches not inns. It seemed wrong
for people to quoif their pints of ale whilst sitting on seats
that had once flanked the aisles of fine looking churches
such as St James, Chinkton Green. Casting forlorn and
watery eyes around the bar, Egbert spotted a darkened
corner where he might sit and pass a little of his eternity
observing some of the customers. He had no sooner settled himself than he felt a blast of cold air, as the front door
burst open, a group of locals crashed their way in and
made their way to the bar.

'Hello Doris. How's your luck? Cold enough for you,
Harold?' shouted Bill, a short, fat man with a choleric
complexion, who was wearing an anorak that would have
sat more comfortably on a six foot gorilla.

'Mustn't grumble,' muttered Harold, edging passed his
ample wife to get to the beer taps. 'Pints of bitter is it?'

Bill rubbed his hands. 'Pints of bitter lads?'

'Cheers mate,' they chorused, knocking over some empty beer mugs as they jostled among themselves.

'Watch what you're doin'!' warned Doris, touching her blonded hair and revealing considerable cleavage as she bent to clear the mess.

Bill clutched her heavily bangled arm. 'When,' he wheezed, licking mauve, lips, 'do us boys get the pleasure of your company?'

'Shush! You keep your voice down.' She turned to Harold. 'How long is it now, love, since we played the clubs?'

'Long time ago now, Doll.'

'But 'ow long since we done our song routines?'

'Never mind the song. What about a spot of your special dancing, Doll?' Bill winked, unzipped his anorak and wriggled his barrel chest.

'Tell you what,' said Doris, her voice reduced to a smoky rasp, 'I'll give you a song and a bit of a dance when we're finished 'ere tonight, if you like.'

Harold flushed but said nothing, while the lads, seeing the three of them in conference, whistled and stamped their feet.

'Shush! Not so loud,' cautioned Doris, flapping plump hands. She scratched a red nailed finger down Bill's drip dry shirt. 'It'll cost you.'

'Ah, don't be mean,' he pouted. 'How much?'

'That depends.' Her eyes locked onto his.

Harold drew her to one side. 'Must you, Doll?'

'It's only the chaps, Harold. And it puts a bit extra in our pockets.'

'There's the ghost tours. We do all right, Doll with the ghost tours. There's no need to – well, you know – demean yourself.'

'The ghost tours is not doing so well – the awkward bugger never shows up, does 'e? We may as well cash in while the goin's good.'

'Yes, but stripping at your age – not very nice is it?'

'Fifty-one isn't old. Come on,' she cajoled, giving his

moustache a playful tug. 'Lighten up. The boys like me, even if I am a bit ripe. And anyway, since when 'ave you objected to me bringin' in the loot? Helps pay for our holidays in Benidorm and more besides if I give um a bit extra. Don't pull them faces. Get real! It's the twenty-first century, love. So stop your moanin'.'

'But what if the authorities find out what goes on after hours, we could get closed down.'

'Well, they won't find out if you keep your trap shut. Besides, we got "a lock in" and late licensing permission, so what's wrong wiv that? That's all clear and above board. They're an invited audience, so just think of it as a club, darlin'. It's just a bit of fun, only difference is – we're getting paid for it.'

She turned to Bill. 'I'll see you later, love – usual place. All right? And remember,' nodding at his mates, 'only bring that lot wiv you, understand? Keep your mouths shut – an' we won't have no trouble.'

He gave her a nod and another wink which set the nerve in his right eye twitching. 'You're a babe, Doris – one of the best. Don't have any lady friends you could invite along?'

'One more word out of you sunbeam, and there won't be no more drinkin' after hours. My entertainment is extra. You can take it or leave it, but don't you go getting too greedy now.' She waggled her hips and gave one of her coarse laughs, while Harold slunk off to collect the empties. He had heard enough. How she could degrade herself beat him. Dancing was one thing, but spreading herself about, and there was, he had to admit, plenty to spread, was more than he could stomach. She seemed to like it, that was the trouble. At first it was the cash, and he had to admit, they had needed the cash at the start when things were hard and there were more back payments than they could cope with but not now. She didn't have to do it now. Trouble was Doll liked sex. Loved it, couldn't get enough of it and he was no good, not anymore, not since his operation.

Harold noticed a young couple had come in, opening

and closing the front door with exaggerated care and looking around mystified. Must be strangers. Egbert noticed them too. Now Harold was taking them to sign their names in the register. Could they be Egbert's emissaries, he wondered; the two young people Adelina had spoken of? If they were, then his possible release was imminent and he must set about preparing himself for his big ordeal. If there was to be a séance, he should brush up on his materialisation skills, make himself visible. Recently he had felt too depressed to generate into anything more than an amorphous mass. It was quite true that Doris' ghost tours were not doing so well of late. He was fed up with satisfying that woman's greed by making himself visible to all and sundry. She was a vulture of the first order and the sooner he was out of here the better.

While Harold escorted the two young guests to their rooms, Egbert concentrated on an elderly married couple chatting in the pew opposite. The man possessed an ecclesiastical air. If he were a clergyman, he might appreciate a materialisation. It might strengthen his faith – give him something to take home to his congregation.

'Another drink, Sheila?' Egbert heard George ask.

'No, thanks. I'd better not have anymore.'

'Pleasant little inn. I rather like these old places with their quintessential oak beams and inglenook fireplaces.'

She smiled and took hold of George's hand. 'I'm so glad we came. The break has done you good.' It was true; the change in him was nothing short of remarkable. But this extraordinary transition dated, not from the advent of their holiday but back to that Sunday afternoon in October when he had smelt the strange apples. Here now, was a man who no longer snored, rose cheerful in the mornings, sang around the house, helped with household chores and was affectionate into the bargain. Sharing the same bed once more had resurrected their sex lives and Sheila was left with a sense of well being she had forgotten existed.

'Sheila!' George sat bolt upright.

'What?'

'Look! Over there – sitting by the far window. A man in black.'

'I can't see a man in black.'

'Yes, you can.'

'I can't, I tell you. Anyway, what about him?'

'He's looking at us.'

'Perhaps he knows you.'

He gripped her arm. 'I don't believe this.'

'Don't believe what? Make sense George'

But George said nothing – just stared.

'You don't believe what? Let go of my arm.'

'Oh.' He flopped back in his seat. 'He's gone!' He drained his glass. 'I need another of these.'

'Strikes me, you have had enough whisky for one night.'

'It's not the drink, Sheila. I was looking over there, by that leaded window that looks out over the lake … it was so weird. A trick of the light perhaps or …'

'Or what?'

'Do you believe in ghosts, Sheila?'

'Of course not.'

'Well, whatever it was that I saw, well, it materialised, became something, someone.'

'How could it possibly?'

'It was like some kind of tremor; a tremor that formed itself into matter.'

'Go on.'

'It became this man, dressed in black.'

'George!'

'No, really. He was wearing eighteenth century clothes and …' he stopped. 'Don't look at me like that, Sheila.'

'Like what?'

'Like I'm mad, or something.'

'I'm sorry, darling. I want to believe you but …'

'I know. It sounds outlandish and me a priest as well.'

'What happened next?'

'This spectre, or whatever it was, smiled, bowed and then vanished. It was so strange because while this was going on, everything around me went totally quiet and you can hear how noisy it is in here.'

'Come on, darling, we had better be going. You have had a fright.'

'Do you know,' he said, as he followed her out. 'In a strange way, I feel almost uplifted. I want to come back to The Black Dog Inn before we leave on Monday. Perhaps I can find out the history of this place from the landlords.'

Sheila pointed to a notice pinned to the entrance: 'Come and meet our resident ghost. Tours twice weekly, subject to demand. Bookings via Harold and Doris. Seeing is believing.'

'Must be your lucky day, George. You've "seen" for nothing.' She nudged him playfully. 'But do you believe? That's the point.'

George didn't answer.

🌼 🌼

Egbert was furious. How dare Thomas upstage him like this; it was not easy materialising, especially in noisy conditions such as these. But Thomas just had to get in first – be the clever one and steal his pitch. This was not the first time he had seen him lurking around either. What was he up to? The man had always been a shady character, right back to those early days at the manor when he'd employed him as Adelina's dancing instructor. It had not taken Thomas long to worm his way into his wife's bed either. But Egbert had turned a blind eye to all that. Being impotent, it was the easiest and most convenient way of handling a tricky and sensitive situation. As he could not satisfy his wife's sexual appetite, Thomas filled the slot. He had not wanted it, of course; the thought of that man sleeping with his wife turned his stomach; gave him ulcers. And even now, years after their deaths, he had a niggling suspicion that this chicaner was duping him. But what could he do about it, stuck up here as he was?

Steeling himself, Egbert left his pew and glided over to

the far window, the better to confront him. 'Greetings to you, Thomas!'

'Sir Egbert!'

'What a coincidence, finding you here.'

'Well I ...'

'I have seen you several times, Thomas, and yet you have not seen me. Curious that. You must know I reside here, albeit against my will, and yet you repeatedly choose to ignore me. Is that the way to treat a former employer?'

'Sir Egbert!'

'And how is my wife? You are in touch, I take it.' He was trembling with rage.

'No need to get prickly, Sir Egbert. I see her on occasion, yes. Our last meeting was in the manor library, if you must know. And what is more, she was feeling a good deal warmer, thanks to my help.'

'And her feet?'

'The same, I fear.'

'But were you not teaching her to glide or some such thing?'

'I have been most awfully busy, Sir Egbert.'

'Then if you are so busy, why are you up here giving materialisations?' There! Better to get it out.

'As it happens,' said Thomas, eyebrows raised, 'I am thinking of changing my job.'

'Really? But I thought that you enjoyed your work as a guide.'

'I do. It is just that I seek more ...'

'More what?'

'Recognition.'

Egbert gave a dry laugh. 'That follows.'

'There is no need to take that attitude, Sir Egbert. Now, if you will allow me to be of assistance, it could be to our mutual advantage.'

Egbert eyed him narrowly. What had he up his sleeve? he wondered.

'I know all about the séance,' said Thomas, a touch self-righteously.

'Adelina told you, I suppose.'

'She has briefed me, yes.'

'She has briefed you,' Egbert mimicked, jealousy stabbing his gut. 'Pity I am not briefed more. Still,' he sighed, 'I think she has not been herself since the fire, or since her eviction from that curate's house.' He paused, 'You know about the manor fire, I suppose?'

Thomas bowed his head. 'A most unfortunate accident.'

'Gave her a bit of a knock, did that. Since then she has not been in touch with me as much as I would like. Thought transmission is damnably poor, you know.' Perhaps, on second thoughts, it was wiser not to apportion too much blame. Thomas was clever and manipulative: a potential advocate and one that he could, in these present circumstances, ill afford to lose.

'Look, Sir Egbert,' Thomas placated, adjusting his 'boot' cuff. 'I apologise for giving that materialisation. Ill mannered of me, I know, but I wanted to see if I was still in good working order.'

Sir Egbert grunted.

'That young couple ...'

'Freddie and Sophie?'

'The very same. They have arrived,' said Thomas.

'Ah! I thought so.'

'Tomorrow, they will ask Doris and Harold's permission to hold a séance. Let us hope they agree to it.'

'Amen to that.'

'Tell me Sir Egbert: what do you seriously think are your chances of getting out of here?'

'Without the help of our young friends, no chance at all. I am exploited here to the hilt.'

'Is that so?' said Thomas, feigning surprise.

'For a fee, visitors are taken to the "cold spots," the areas I am supposed to haunt. Doris invents stories about me that change by the week. No doubt,' he grumbled, seeing Thomas smirk, 'you think this is all highly amusing.'

'Indeed, no. Pray continue.'

'The public seldom see me these days. I just bang about

a bit and they go away. Irritates Doris no end. She likes me to appear, give them all their monies' worth, but I won't, I can't anyway at the moment, I feel so depleted.' He lowered his voice. 'Then of course, there is the other business.'

'What other business?'

'Doris' other little money spinner.'

'Oh?'

'Occasionally, a small number of the male fraternity are invited into the "back room," as she calls it, for drinks and entertainment after hours.'

'What sort of entertainment?'

'Once the men are in their cups …'

'Drunk, yes?'

'She removes her clothes.'

Thomas roared with laughter.

'I do not see anything to laugh at.'

'What fine sport! The thought of that fat, blowzy woman taking her clothes off is too funny for words. Is there music?'

'Yes. It is a strip tease act with singing and dancing.'

'And that is it?'

'Not always, no.'

'Pray, go on.'

'That I will not.'

Thomas wiped his eyes. 'What merriment.'

'I can quite see,' Egbert said sourly, 'why an old reprobate like yourself finds such sordid goings on amusing.'

'Sordid? Nonsense. The woman is resourceful. What is wrong with that? I tell you this fits in splendidly with my plans. When is the next entertainment?'

'Tonight after closing. Why?'

'No matter. Now, back to business. My proposal.'

'Yes, Thomas, your proposal please.'

'I am going to provide you with a plan B.'

'Plan B?'

'Should plan A fail, I will offer to replace you – hence Plan B. What do you say to that?'

Egbert's mouth drooped. 'You mean to say that you would be willing to come to this God forsaken inn? But why?'

'Because Sir Egbert, if I were their resident ghost, I could move away from my present job which is quietly driving me potty and into the world of entertainment. And who knows? If I were to find another ghost with my potential, we could join forces: we could expand.'

Egbert stared at him stunned.

'I could turn this second rate, tatty little inn into one of the most successful restaurants in the country.'

'I see,' returned Egbert slowly. 'And how do you propose to implement your plan?'

'If your appeal should fail, and I rather fear that it may, I will appear at the séance and put in my offer. Once Doris and Harold realise that I mean business, I believe they will give their consent for you to leave. Once that is given, an important factor, Freddie and Sophie can use their psychic power to release your spirit, so that you can return to the manor.'

'Have you told Adelina all this?'

'Not exactly.' Examining his fingernails. 'I fear that I am not in her good books at present.'

Egbert's mouth began to twitch.

'I owe her gliding lessons, you see.'

'Of course,' snapped Egbert, 'her inability to glide ensures she stays put, does it not? And that suits you very well, at least for the present, until some better ghost, a younger model perhaps, comes along. Am I not right?'

'Sir Egbert!'

'Do not play the innocent with me, Thomas. I know what you are about.'

'What I am about? I will tell you what I am about, Sir Egbert, I am about to save your soul.'

'Come, Thomas. You think I do not know what has been going on at the manor between you and my Adelina?'

Thomas blanched. 'Look here, Sir Egbert, do you want my help, or do you not?'

'I suppose so,' he returned sulkily.

'Very well. Then I shall overlook your harsh words and proceed. Now, once the séance has commenced, I want you to materialise, do you understand?'

'I know all that.' Tapping his foot.

'Listen, please. Once you have appeared, you will state your case and wait for the landlord's response. Should it prove unfavourable, I too will manifest and put forward my proposal.'

'To take my place?'

'Yes. Plan B. Pretty good, eh?'

'You were always very sure of yourself, Thomas.' Oh, to have the pleasure of denting that ego! He felt so tired, so done in with it all. 'I must rest,' he said. 'My light dims.'

Thomas rose to his feet. Although shorter than Egbert, his carriage was more imposing – his back straighter, his head more erect. 'Until the séance, then.'

'Until the séance. And thank you, Thomas.' The words nearly choked him, but he supposed this contingency plan was worth a try. Besides, it was churlish to appear ungrateful.

Once Thomas had vanished, Egbert left the bar and glided upstairs.

He felt sickened by the noise, the stink of beer and strong cheese: of spineless Harold, and Doris with her cheap jewellery and uncouth talk.

He passed Sophie and Freddie on the landing, but even for them he could not summon enough energy to make himself visible. Pity, he would like to have introduced himself. Continuing along the corridor, passed the bedrooms – each named after a lake – he reached a bathroom that housed a roomy, warm airing cupboard: soft with blankets, towels, freshly laundered sheets and Harold's drip dry shirts. Lowering his head, he crept inside, settled himself next to the water tank, closed his eyes and put out his light.

 eleven

'Give it to me baby, baby,' crooned Doris, swinging generous hips in time to canned music. 'Ignite me with your love tonight.'

She was ablaze in a dress of red sequins, figure hugging tight and held together at the front with a strip of Velcro.

'Thrill me with your voice, then maybe –' Her breasts rippled and heaved. 'Baby, we'll make dynamite.'

'She's fuckin' useless, man.' Bill's mate from Trinidad, stubbed his cigar butt into a sand ashtray.

'I think I'll go home to the wife,' said another. 'Get more of a thrill out of her than this one.'

Bill said nothing. They had a point. Doris had gone off the boil. Her voice, once rich and resonant was now strident and flat: her voluptuous figure no longer sexy but fat.

'All right boys?' she called, pre-empting approval with little becks of the head.

'Get a move on, Doris,' grumbled Bill looking at his watch. He had fifteen fruit machines to empty first thing.

'Yeh, come on gel,' shouted a beery voice from the back, 'Show us your boobs.'

'Be patient boys.' She tottered across to the stereo recorder as fast as her stiletto heels would permit and changed the tape. A few seconds later a tinny rendering of *The Stripper* blared out.

'Not thith again, Dorith,' piped a whiskered youth with a lisp, as he staggered to the bar. 'We had thith latht time.'

'Yeh!' chorused the others, beginning a slow handclap.

Doris shrugged her shoulders slithered over to Bill, pinched his face until it resembled a squeezed lemon, then proceeded to express similar displays of affection at the other tables. She stroked hair, sat on laps, pulled ties and blew kisses. This titillation complete, the scene was set for her to remove her dress by way of the Velcro. The tape jammed. Roars of protest, followed by a mass exodus to the bar where Harold, bearing a look of pained acceptance, served them all with luke warm beer.

Doris found a pencil, untangled the tape and rewound it to the beginning of the number. Waiting until the men were reseated, she turned the volume to maximum, took up position 'centre stage,' and gave the rest of the act her all. Had she tempered her performance with a little more restraint – fewer contortions, wiggles and wriggles – it might not have happened. But it was her back bend that did it. An ear piercing shriek was the signal for Harold to leave his post, rush to her side, lie on his back to gain access to hers, and manipulate it at the exact spot that rendered her upright. This done, he escorted his wife off the floor, ordered everyone to go home, and taking her arm, led her, hobbling, moaning and cursing up to bed.

No one had noticed the handsome figure in black, sitting cross-legged under the Exit sign. Only Harold, switching off the lights, fancied he heard the faint sound of laughter in the dark.

🌿 🌿

The room behind the bar served as an office and housed boxes of crisps, a computer and an old, roll top desk. Freddie, Sophie and Harold were seated around a circular table by the window. Perched on Harold's head sat Joey, a blue and grey budgerigar, who had the disconcerting habit of suddenly taking flight and making low level dives over Freddie's head. In a nearby armchair and propped up with cushions sat Doris, newspapers, cigarettes and chocolates ready to hand.

'Three sisters in Hydesville, New York, formally started Spiritualism,' began Freddie, referring to some notes he had made for the occasion. 'They claimed to make contact with the spirits by a series of rappings.'

'Is that so?' Doris winced, as she leaned forward for a cigarette. 'It's all very interesting dear, but what exactly are we driving at here? Harold, offer these young people drinks.'

'This coffee's just fine, thanks,' said Freddie, draining his cup. Whatever else, he must keep a clear head.

'I'll 'ave a brandy thanks, Harold – and make it a double. Might settle the pain.'

'How did you hurt your back?' asked Sophie, trying to be friendly.

'I was kneelin' by my bed dear, saying me prayers.' She winked at Harold who wore the same pained look as the night before.

Doris bit into a chocolate then drew on her cigarette. 'Thank Gawd the church bells 'ave stopped. Drive you crackers.'

'It is a Sunday morning, dear,' handing her her drink. 'The church is entitled to advertise of a Sunday. It's their job.'

'Talking of advertising,' said Freddie, spotting an opening, 'Sophie and I have read about your ghost tours.'

'That's why you're 'ere, isn't it love?' said Doris, picking a piece of nut from her front tooth.

He stared at her astounded. Had Adelina been in touch with her? And where was Adelina now? That's what he'd like to know. It seemed she had gone again – left the curate's house for good. Well, he just hoped that their intuition would see him and Sophie through the rest of the weekend.

'You should see your face,' laughed Doris. 'Don't worry. We wouldn't let you travel all this way for nothin', would we, Harold?'

'Mm? No, 'course not.'

''Ow much?'

'I'm sorry?' Freddie.

'For the interview ... 'ow much?'

'You think we're the press?' Sophie stared, stunned.

'Well aren't you?'

'No, we are not.'

'Then who are you?' asked Harold.

'The Inland Revenue!' shrieked Doris. 'Show them the books, Harold. We've nothing to hide.'

Freddie said, 'We're not from the Inland,' and looked helplessly at Sophie.

Doris held out her glass. 'Harold? Another brandy. I mustn't stiffen.'

'We are a kind of emissary,' explained Sophie, who rather liked the sound of the word.

'Say again?' Doris picking another chocolate.

'Your ghost,' said Freddie. 'The one who haunts this inn …'

'We thought you was the press,' grumbled Harold, under his breath.

'What about our ghost?' snapped Doris.

'Sophie and I are mediums,' said Freddie, ducking from another of Joey's dives.

'Harold, put that bloody bird back in its cage. Mediums, you say?'

'That is correct.' He would introduce a note of formality into his voice: that might redress the balance. 'We have reason to believe that your ghost is displaced.'

Doris looked blank. 'Displaced? What you on about?'

'I mean, he doesn't belong here, he belongs somewhere else.'

'Chinkton Manor,' said Sophie. 'That's where he belongs. And he wants desperately to go back there.'

'Now I get it.' drawled Doris. 'That fancy speech you made earlier was leading up to all this, wasn't it?'

Harold handed Doris her brandy then made a grab for Joey.

'A displaced ghost, eh? Well, well. So you think that Harold and me is keeping the old boy against his will.'

'Yes, we do,' said Sophie, disliking Doris more by the minute.

'Who sent you – 'is wife?' Her cackle sent Joey squawk-ing across the room, scattering Freddie's notes and a flurry of fine feathers over the floor.

'As a matter of fact, yes.' Sophie, firm, unsmiling.

'You're nuts!'

'Her name,' continued Freddie, wishing he had never come, 'is Adelina, and she was, is, the resident ghost of Chinkton Manor, Chinkton Green. She lived there with her husband, Sir Egbert Wilham, in the eighteenth centu-ry. So you see, Chinkton Manor is his rightful Seat not The Black Dog Inn. It's simple really.' Flushed with embarrass-ment, he leant down to pick up his papers, thankful for something to do.

Doris was thoughtful: she liked a nice title. 'Sir, did you say he was a sir?'

'That's right – Sir Egbert Wilham. He wants to be reunit-ed with his wife and home. It's only natural, don't you think?' Trying to appeal to her better nature.

'If 'es so un'appy – this Sir Egbert, why doesn't 'e vanish back to where 'e come from?'

'Because he can't,' said Sophie, 'at least, not without your permission. Once that has been granted we, as mediums, can help him on his way.'

'You mean 'es stuck?' Doris sucked her teeth and smirked.

'In a sense – yes.'

'What we would like to do,' said Sophie, with an enthusi-asm Freddie wished he shared, 'is for the four of us to hold a séance in the hope that Sir Egbert will materialise and state his case.'

'Well, that's a new one on me. Never been to one of them before. What you say, Harold?'

Harold chose only to shake his head. He preferred not to dwell on the supernatural – not after what he'd seen.

'All right, we're game,' said Doris, 'but it won't make no difference. Business is business and we can't afford to lose 'im.'

'All we ask is for you to give him a fair hearing,' said

Freddie hopefully.

'All right. Can't do no 'arm. Be quite a laugh to pay our respects. 'E's a temperamental old bugger. Never seen 'im meself, but you saw 'im once, didn't you love, whilst you was puttin' away the sheets.'

Harold shuddered and said nothing. A terrible thing it was to meet a ghost in your own airing cupboard.

Doris looked at her watch. 'We'll 'ave the séance this afternoon at two o'clock sharp. I'll shut shop for one hour and one hour only. Sunday's good for trade, although in this cold weather we don't get the customers same as normal.' She shrugged. 'But one hour's our limit, under-stood?'

'Thank you, Doris,' said Freddie, relieved to have come this far. 'And may we use this office? Your circular table is ideal for holding a sitting.'

'If that's what you want.' Doris clutched her back, heaved herself out of the chair and staggered to the door. 'But this "ad better be good, folks.'

As she left the room with Harold porter to her cigarettes, chocolates and bottle of brandy, Freddie and Sophie were left wondering what they had let themselves in for.

twelve

'Doris won't be long,' whispered Harold, hovering outside the office. 'She's just putting the finishing touches to her hair.' He rubbed his hands. 'Chilly already, wouldn't you say?'

'Come in, Harold,' said Freddie.

'Yes, come in,' urged Sophie. 'Don't stand by the door.'

He placed a cautious toe over the threshold as though testing the water for crabs then glanced fretfully over his shoulder. 'She's not herself is Doll – not since doing her back in. Go easy on her.'

'Harold!' screeched Doris, from somewhere in the upper regions. 'Come and zip me up.'

'Excuse me, you two.' He withdrew his toe. 'Coming, Doll.'

'You're so calm, Sophie,' said Freddie, after he'd gone. 'I wish I'd half your confidence.'

She stroked his cheek. 'Try not to worry. It'll be all right-you'll see.'

Five minutes later saw the arrival of Doris, dramatic in full-length hyacinth satin, her blonde hair piled high.

'Doris!' Freddie exclaimed, thinking there was an almost gruesome beauty about her. 'You look, you look well, eh, very striking.'

She beamed. 'Where do you want us love?'

'Right. I'd like us round this table; so you sit next to Harold. Now you, Sophie, and then me.'

'Where's Joey?' Harold cast dejected eyes around the room. 'Shouldn't we put him in his cage? He'll be petrified.'

'Oh leave the wretched thing,' cranked Doris, lowering her bottom onto one of the high-backed chairs. ''E's up there on the curtain rail.' She winced. 'Bring me a cushion, love.'

'Now,' directed Freddie, 'in a few moments we will place our hands on the table, fingers touching. That way we combine our energy forces and there is more chance of making contact with the other side.'

'A bit spooky eh, Doll?' Harold muttered, placing a plump cushion behind her back.

'It's important,' cautioned Freddie, 'that there's as little disruption as possible once the séance gets under way. Too much noise could frighten away the spirits.'

Harold's eyebrows shot up in alarm. 'How many do you reckon on coming then?'

Freddie shrugged. 'Who can say? One of us might go into trance and one or more spirit might use our vocal chords to speak through us, or there again, messages might come via the air. There is, of course, no guarantee that we will see Sir Egbert, or any other spirit for that matter. It depends on how much ectoplasm he is able to generate – that's if he decides to use ectoplasm, of course.'

'You don't need me, Doll.' Harold wheezed. 'Tell you what, I'll go and make us a nice cup of tea for the interval.'

Doris clapped a steely hand on his arm. 'Stay where you are. We need you to add to this energy thing. Just breathe nice and slow and you'll be fine. What's this with the ectoplasm, Freddie?'

'Ectoplasm is composed, either of white vapour, or a milky like substance that is quite thick and oily in texture. To create a materialisation, the spirit sometimes takes this ectoplasm that can mysteriously exude from either the medium's mouth, ears or nose, and builds it into a human form that we can recognise.'

'Does it stain?' Doris had just had a new dralon cover put on her easy chair.

'I don't think so.' Freddie wished they would stop asking him questions.

'What about light?' she went on. 'Shouldn't we close the curtains and light a candle? That's what they do in the films, isn't it?'

'That won't be necessary. What might be a good idea though, is to say a short prayer before we begin, it will help keep the evil spirits at bay.'

Harold jumped to his feet. 'Right, that's it. You can count me out.'

Sophie leaned over and touched his hand. 'There's really no need to be scared. You're quite safe.' Her voice seemed to calm him a little and he resumed his seat.

Freddie closed his eyes and recited a short prayer that he remembered from his school days, then the four of them placed their hands tentatively on the table.

'Does anyone mind if I smoke?'

'Not now Doll,' muttered Harold, between his teeth.

''Ow long before we witness some action then?'

Freddie started to sweat. 'We have to be patient, Doris. Sir Egbert, are you there, Sir Egbert?'

Silence.

'Is there any one out there?'

Still nothing.

'Look folks,' said Doris after a couple of minutes, 'Let's give it a miss, shall we? my back's playing up.'

'Shush,' said Harold. 'Listen!'

'What?' Doris.

'That noise.'

'What noise? I don't 'ear no noise.'

'That knocking.'

'It's that bloody bird up on the window rail.'

'No, Harold's right,' said Freddie. 'It's coming from over by the door. Quiet everyone, please! Is there anyone out there? Answer us.'

They waited. Sophie, gripping Freddie's hand, Doris, her mouth shiny and slack and Harold, staring, his eyes like saucers.

'Is that you Sir Egbert?' Sophie.

Two more knocks – louder. She glanced at Freddie who mouthed for her to continue.

'Do you have a message for us?'

Knock. Knock.

She spoke to the others. 'What do we do now?'

'You're the mediums,' shrugged Doris. 'You sort it out.'

'We could try going into trance, Sophie,' suggested Freddie.

'Yes, it'll give Sir Egbert the chance to speak through us, especially if he can't make himself visible.'

''Ang on a minute,' said Doris. 'What are we supposed to do while you two nod off? Get out the crystal ball?'

'Just bear with us, please,' implored Freddie. 'And remember – no noise.'

He and Sophie sat back in their chairs and closed their eyes. But Freddie found it impossible to empty his mind, he was too on edge and the musky scent Doris was wearing made him feel a bit sick. Perhaps it would help if he focused his mind on the picture of Sir Egbert that hung outside Lady Wilham's bedroom.

Sophie's thoughts went out to Adelina. She just hoped and prayed that she was all right and hadn't got herself into anymore trouble.

Doris reckoned that if Freddie and Sophie could close their eyes, she might as well get a bit of shut-eye too. Was this all there was to it then: a couple or so raps? Bloody waste of time. If they thought she was going to give up Egbert, they had another think coming. 'Appy or not, he was theirs for keeps and it gave her a nice warm feeling in the pit of her stomach to think that her and Harold's opinion could influence his so called vibrations.

Harold had no intention of closing his eyes. There was no knowing what might happen with his blinkers shut. He glanced at the others. They looked fast asleep. Now, if he was to move ever so quiet, one step at a time, he could be out of here and none of them the wiser. He gave an involuntary shudder, as gingerly, soundlessly he rose from his seat and tiptoed towards the door. This part of the room felt colder than usual – much colder, and he drew his jacket close. It was then he saw it. There, standing to the left of the door, the very door Harold walked through every day of his working life stood an angel. He knew it was an angel because he was all lit up like the Blackpool illuminations. He was quite old as angels go and there was something strangely familiar about him. He was dressed, not in a white gown with wings and a halo, but in funny old-fashioned clothes like you sometimes saw at Christmas on the front of fancy chocolate boxes.

Harold's teeth began to chatter. He quivered, he shook. He shook so violently he felt he had been plugged into the main's socket. Slowly, very slowly, the angel started to move. He drew closer and closer, until Harold was staring into his large, luminous eyes. And then suddenly and with an almighty whoosh, the angel passed straight through him and onto the other side.

'Greetings to you all,' he said, gliding towards the others. 'I am Sir Egbert Wilham,'

'Strewth!' cried Doris, opening her eyes.

'Wonderful!' chorused Sophie and Freddie.

'Help!' quaked Harold, as he stood shivering by the door.

'Please, be quick,' pleaded Egbert, his voice distant and frail. 'I do not have long.'

Freddie cleared his throat and swallowed hard. 'Right. We are gathered here this afternoon, to establish whether Sir Egbert Wilham, previous address: Chinkton Manor, Chinkton Green, wants to return to his rightful baronial seat, or remain here, at The Black Dog Inn. Am I correct, Sir Egbert?'

He inclined his head.

'It seems, however,' Freddie continued, 'that certain members present are not happy with this arrangement. Is that not so, Doris?'

She nodded and pursed her lips. 'Now, Sir Egbert, why do you want to go and leave us? Aren't you 'appy here? We thought you was 'appy with us.'

'How can you say that?' Sophie cut in heatedly.

'Calm down, will you?' Freddie whispered. 'Egbert has to be asked.'

'You know we love 'avin' you live with us,' Doris fawned.

'Love having the money, you mean,' said Sophie, under her breath.

'Cool it,' hissed Freddie

'Well, she's so two faced.'

'Two faced, am I? I'll have you know, my girl, that we've 'elped and supported your Sir Egbert. When 'e was first plonked down 'ere – none of our doin' note, 'e was made to feel real welcome. 'Ow many people do you know what would put up wiv a ghost in their midst? But we loved 'im from the start, didn't we Harold? Harold? What you doin' by the door? Come and sit down.'

'Sir Egbert,' implored Freddie, a note of panic entering his voice, 'will you please tell us what you want to do.'

Harold, sobbing quietly, tiptoed back to his seat, while Egbert, his energy depleted by Doris' presence, began to stutter. Perhaps he should have used ectoplasm, although he doubted that it would have helped. Besides the stuff smelt of ozone and made him feel light-headed.

'I ...' he began.

'Yes?'

'I w...'

'Yes?'

'I want t ... to go h ... home.'

'And you are unhappy here?'

'Y – y – yes.'

Freddie heaved a great sigh. 'Thank you. Thank you so much.'

Then turning to Harold and Doris, 'You have witnessed Sir Egbert's request to return to his manor. So what do you say? Will you let him go?'

Silence. Then Doris slammed her fat fist on the table. 'No!'

'Oh, come on love.' Harold, who was working up fresh courage to leave the room and if necessary the country, could think of nothing he'd like better than to see the back of him.

'Whose side are you on?' she barked.

'It's not a question of sides, dear. But it's not right to keep a ghost against his will.'

'Have you spoken with your wife recently, Sir Egbert?' asked Freddie. 'We don't seem able to get in touch with her.'

'N ... n ... no.'

'Perhaps,' Sophie suggested, 'if we were to sit and concentrate our minds, we might reach her. She could tell us what to do next.'

'Concentrate all you like dears, it won't make no difference. 'E doesn't 'ave our permission to leave and that's final.'

'Doris, love.'

'Shut up Harold. I know what I'm doin'.'

Egbert moaned. He knew he could not leave without the landlord's permission. Even with Freddie and Sophie's help, he would be unable to move. Negativity, such as the kind Doris poured into the atmosphere was enough to shatter his fragile electro vibrations. The mere sight of the woman depressed him. From where could he muster his strength? Consent, willingly given, was what was needed. That would raise his spirits, infect him with hope and charge him with energy. He looked around in desperation. Where was Thomas? It was time for Plan B. So where was he? If he did not show up soon, it would be too late; he would have to stay here forever, until the inn crumbled to the ground. To be reliant on one's wife's lover was humiliating enough, but reliant he was. There was no getting away from it, Egbert needed help, and needed it fast.

thirteen

Adelina was trapped. Not in a forest, or a park, or even in hell, but in Chinkton Manor Maze. With daylight came this realisation and with it feelings of relief and frustration. Relief at finding herself on familiar ground – she recognised the chimney pots and the manor roof – and frustration for lacking the courage and the wherewithal to get out.

It was three days now since she had lost her way on her return journey from seeing Maurice, and with time on her hands, she brooded and worried in turn. Brooded over what she now deemed a selfish act of malice for stealing the urn in the first place and worried, because she had left the parcel in the costume department. Simon would never forgive her for that. Perhaps this boscage was to be her final resting-place – her punishment.

Adelina sat on a wooden garden seat and stared up at the yew hedge: high, thick and impenetrable. Calm, she must remain calm: relax her mind, allow her thoughts to drift to the north, to The Black Dog Inn.

She closed her eyes and concentrated and not a moment too soon. For now she could see that the séance was in progress and things were not going well. Egbert looked drained, ill and agitated. Freddie and Sophie, tense and on edge. There was some nasty negativity coming from Doris, and Harold was shaking like a leaf. This was not good: not good at all.

Should she make her presence felt: tell them where she was? No. She must be patient. It would be wiser – more circumspect to lie low for the present. For with Doris digging in her heels, the less they knew of her whereabouts the better. She must think of a means of escape certainly, but for now she needed every bit of cosmic energy she could muster.

Ø Ø

Thomas bided his time. Sir Egbert, or no Sir Egbert, he refused to be hurried. He was watching Doris: restive, impatient, nicotine deprived. As tensions mounted, so did her craving. When he thought she could bear it no longer, he drew a deep, spiritual breath then gently, without disturbing the others, made himself visible. He touched her lightly on the shoulder.

'Cor blimey!' she said, 'Who are you?'

Who, indeed! The others stared, wide-eyed: Harold making little whimpering noises while Thomas concentrated all his prescient powers on a packet of cigarettes and a gold lighter that lay unclaimed on the bar next door. Within moments they dropped with precision timing into his outstretched hand. 'Cigarette, madam?' he said.

Doris, her mouth agape, grabbed one greedily. 'Thanks ever so, I must have left mine upstairs.'

'Don't touch them,' shrieked Harold. 'They might be poison!'

'Oh shut up!' She placed it between her lips, accepted a light and inhaled with smoker's satisfaction, drawing the smoke deep into her lungs. 'See!' she wheezed, brushing ash off her front, 'The spirits don't object to a quiet smoke.'

'Oh my God!' wailed Harold, and rushed from the room.

'What's up wiv 'im?' But Doris had what she wanted and didn't much care.

Freddie turned to Sophie. 'Are you all right?' he whispered. 'Not frightened.'

'I love it. Who would have thought – two materialisations at our first séance?'

'Yes, but who is he?' he whispered.

'Allow me to introduce myself. My name is Thomas – friend and advisor to Sir Egbert and Lady Wilham. May I proceed Sir Egbert?'

'Oh, p ... p ... please.' He was growing misty around the feet.

'Thomas turned to Doris. 'I have a commercial proposition, madam.'

'Oh, yes?' She settled herself into her chair. Her bad back forgotten.

'As you are aware, Sir Egbert wants to return to Chinkton Manor. Now I understand your reluctance to let him go. Business is business, but what say you to a straight ghost exchange?'

'How do you mean?'

'You run a successful inn here, in Windermere. No doubt people come from miles around to taste your beer.'

'We do dinners and stop overs too, you know.'

'And I am sure you provide an excellent service.'

'We aim to please.' A coy smile.

'Doris. May I call you Doris?'

'Course you can.' He'd nice manners she'd say that for 'im.

'Doris, I want you to listen carefully. Imagine this: A husband and wife glance through a holiday brochure offering weekend breaks, but weekend breaks with a difference. While the average brochure advertises mundane holidays at competitive prices, you, at The Black Dog Inn, do not.'

'We can't afford to do that,' she snapped. 'We 'ave our overheads same as everyone, and we 'ave to break even.'

'Quality comes at a price, Doris. Do not forget that. Now, this couple have always wanted to visit The Lake District; and now that her husband has been given that long awaited pay rise, they can afford to holiday somewhere a little different – a little special. Browsing through the catalogues, they come across your printed brochure, and low and behold, there is a centre-fold picture of our very own Doris, owner and entrepreneur of The Black Dog Inn, inviting them to visit the inn with its own resident ghost.'

'Is that all?' she grimaced. 'We've already got our resident ghost. We've got 'im,' pointing at Egbert who was now very hazy indeed.

'Ah! But this is a resident ghost with a difference. First of all, he is not elusive or temperamental. Do forgive me, Sir Egbert,' he said, addressing the misty blob.

'Oh get on with it bl ... bl ... blast you!'

'This ghost,' continued Thomas, 'is available on demand. He is professional and slick. Secondly, and most importantly, he is a ghost with talent – talent that could be used for profitable gain.'

'What kind of talent?' Her eyes narrowed with mistrust.

'He is an expert at gliding and vanishing. His specialty, as you witnessed earlier, is apports.'

'Say again?'

'Apports. It is from the French word, apporter: to carry. You saw how I produced the cigarettes?'

She nodded. 'We are talking about *you*, I take it?'

'We are. Indeed we are. And Doris, I could perform these feats in front of a paying audience. Could make you and Harold a small fortune.'

She grunted. ''Ow would you organise all this?'

'You would employ the cooks, but the best cooks. Superb dinners would precede my entertainment.'

'But we don't 'ave no theatre.'

'We would erect a stage in the restaurant: your present

dining room.'

'You seen the dining room, have you?'

'Yes, madam, I have seen it.'

'I perform meself sometimes, of an evenin'.'

He smiled politely, resisted the impulse to tell her that he had witnessed the previous night's fiasco. Diplomacy and face-saving went hand in hand.

'I 'ave to admit,' she confided, 'the clients are not what they was and something different might be worth considerin'.' She readjusted her cushion. 'If me and Harold was to agree to your comin', what's the catch?'

'No catch, Doris – just a plain, straight forward ghost exchange.'

'So you want us to release Sir Egbert in exchange for you.'

'That is what I propose.'

'What a wonderful idea!' exclaimed Sophie. 'Solves everything.'

'Great!' cried Freddie.

'Oh, d … d … do be quick,' urged Egbert.

'Yes, do be quick, Doris. What d'you say?' urged Freddie.

'I say, no.'

'But why not?'

'Because I want to keep them both, that's why not.'

'Is that not a mild excessive?' drawled Thomas, who could think of nothing worse than working with his former boss.

'Two is better than one: twice the publicity. More cash.'

'You can't do that,' wailed Sophie.

'Looks like your Sir Egbert will be stayin' with us a while longer,' triumphed Doris, reaching for another cigarette.

'Why you nasty, money grabbing woman!' cried Sophie, jumping to her feet.

Freddie looked pleadingly at Thomas, but he appeared suddenly distracted. His interest in all this had mysteriously evaporated as he kept muttering something about eau de Cologne.

'What's the matter, Thomas?'

'I must go to her at once. Adelina has got lost again,' he

said, gliding swiftly towards the window.

'Adelina? You have made contact with Adelina?'

He nodded.

'Oh, thank goodness for that,' said Sophie. 'But where is she and how do you know she is lost?'

'Your meditation activated her radio waves and transmitted a whiff of her scent. I must leave you now, at once, I have spent too long ignoring her needs.'

'But tell us where she is,' begged Freddie.

'She prefers her whereabouts to be kept secret, for the present.' Thomas bowed. 'Farewell, I shall be back.'

'Do you 'ave to go?' whined Doris. 'Look, if we was to come to some arrangement. Naturally,' she winced, seeing his stern look, 'I wouldn't keep you 'ere against your will.'

He raised a pencil thin eyebrow. 'You most certainly would not, madam.'

'We settled on Doris, remember? Nice and friendly, all right?' She lowered her voice. 'Look dear, what about our deal?'

'There is no deal. Not now – not as things stand.' And drawing his black cloak around him, he faded quickly from sight.

'I hope Adelina will be all right,' frowned Freddie. He felt peculiarly lost without their new ally.

'Oh, look,' cried Sophie, who was close to tears. 'Sir Egbert – he's gone too!'

'Yes,' now putting his arms around her, 'well, we were lucky he stayed with us as long as he did.'

'Real little Samaritans aren't we?' Doris snapped. 'What's it to you anyway?'

'Freddie and I care for Adelina,' Sophie flashed. 'We hate to see spirits distressed.'

'Won't you change your mind Doris?' pleaded Freddie.

'You know,' slowly, stubbing out her cigarette, 'I might be tempted to go to the newspapers with all this. Give the punters a good read of a Sunday mornin'.'

'You wouldn't!' said Freddie, appalled.

'I have to earn a livin', same as everyone. And if Thomas

won't join forces with Sir Egbert, and Sir Egbert continues to act like a damp squid – well,' she shrugged, a smugness settling into her features, 'I might as well make a bit, while I can.'

'Freddie, do something,' implored Sophie.

'Like what? I've done all I can.' He moved back his chair abruptly and stood up.

Doris heaved herself out of her seat. 'Trust Harold to go off just when I need 'im. Well,' she said, hobbling towards the door, 'thanks both for the afternoon's entertainment. I enjoyed meetin' our Sir Egbert.' Then checking her watch, 'Is that the time! Better open up, I suppose.'

Sophie sat down and closed her eyes. She could not bear to look at Doris another minute. What sort of person was she to keep a ghost against his will? After a few moments, her breathing slowed and she felt herself sink deeper and deeper into a state of quiet. She was floating, her body lifted away: away from Doris, the room, the inn to some other place, dark, desolate and cold. Slowly, very gradually, out of this inky well, a black pig emerged: a pig with disk-like snout and flaring nostrils. He chewed on large, thick bones. Funicles of flesh hung from his tusks. Sophie felt his breath, foul and hot against her face. She heard Freddie's voice in the distance; felt his hand on her forehead but could not reach out to him, could not get back, could not move.

Doris stood by the door, her turned up nose creased with disgust, as the room filled with such a rancid stench that Freddie thought he would throw up. He rubbed Sophie's hands. Waves of panic washed over him as he gently lifted her out of the chair and laid her on the floor. He should never have brought her here, never subjected her to this danger. If anything should happen to her … He was about to open the sash window to let in some air, when he felt a trembling under his feet. Within moments the room began to tilt and pitch. Piles of papers slid off the desk. A typewriter clattered to the floor. He clutched at the table but it rocked violently and overturned and Freddie lost his balance and fell. Doris careered across the floor like rubbish down a shoot and landed, screaming, on top of him. Joey took off from the curtain rail and flew squawking around the room, feathers flying everywhere.

'Christ Almighty!' yelled Doris, 'Let's get the hell out of 'ere. Come on!' She tugged at Freddie's shirt. 'Come on! Leave 'er, and come on.'

'Are you crazy? Leave Sophie? Never!'

The floor leaned and lurched, bumped and jarred like some crazy ride at a fair. The walls splintered and cracked, plaster and dust showering them white. The wallpaper curled and frizzed. There were tremors and quakes: deep, penetrative rumblings that shook the room until it seemed the very foundations would rend asunder.

Doris clung to Freddie but he wrenched himself free and crawled towards Sophie but was then forced back, as the carpet ripped itself apart and the floorboards upended. Chaotic gravestones, frightful festoons: prophecies of things to come.

'Look!' screeched Doris, pointing.

Near the upturned table, a thick cloud was rising, yellow and dense. Gaseous vapour curled snake-like towards the ceiling. In the middle of it, Freddie could just make out a single pair of pig's trotters. The mist hovered menacingly for a few seconds then quickly cleared. The floor stopped tilting, the walls stopped shaking, Joey resettled on the curtain rail, and the carpet re-laid itself over the now flattened floorboards. The smell was still there, fetid and foul but now they knew where it was coming from.

A pig, black, with long head, dribbling snout and pointed ears, stood motionless in the middle of the room, his little eyes fixed firmly on Doris. Freddie gasped. 'Bellygod!' But Bellygod was dead – slaughtered years back. Well, there was one sure way of finding out. Slowly, cautiously, he edged closer, and peered at its feet. Yes, there it was – the pig had one white, right, front trotter. This was Bellygod, all right. But what was he doing here? Hang on, Sophie was an animal psychic. Could it be that Sophie had gone into trance and unwittingly raised his spirit?

'Keep quiet, Doris,' warned Freddie, under his breath, as she stood petrified, little gulping sounds coming from the back of her throat. 'Don't panic.' But too late. Even as he spoke, she opened her large red mouth, let out a scream and bolted through the door with Bellygod in hot pursuit.

Rushing into the bar he found the front door wide open and swinging on its hinges. There were no signs of them anywhere. Doris and Bellygod had gone.

'Freddie!' A small voice, a cough, a sigh.

'Sophie!' he cried, running back into the office. 'Thank God! Are you all right? I've been that worried.'

'I've been in trance,' she said, rubbing her eyes. 'At least I think I have.'

He cradled her in his arms. 'I thought that I had lost you.'

'I'm fine. Really. A bit woozy, that's all.' She sat up. 'You don't look so hot though.'

'I'm afraid something awful has happened.'

'Freddie, what is it? You look worried sick.'

'It's Doris.'

'Oh, her!'

'No, listen. This pig. It chased her. They've gone – both of them.'

'What!'

'It materialised and fixed its eyes on Doris, she screamed and it chased her out of the inn. Now they have disappeared.'

She looked at him sharply. 'Was it a large, ugly black pig?'

'Yes. Yes, it was.'

'Freddie, do you think I … Oh, God, no!'

'It's possible. Your animal psychic powers may have dug up old Bellygod – you know, the pig I told you about.'

'The one who ate your grandfather?'

He nodded.

'But how do you know that?'

'One of its front right trotters is white and that was its distinguishing mark. Sophie, I must go after them. If you're really okay, can I leave you?'

She staggered to her feet. 'No chance. I'm coming with you. We're in this together, remember? Oh Freddie, I hope she'll be all right. I feel it's all my fault. She took his hand and together they went into the bar. But she pulled up short when she saw the mess: pictures askew, spilt beer, the open front door fetching a gale that whipped the curtains and sent glasses jangling, and crashing to the floor.

Freddie grabbed a couple of coats that were lying on a chair, and they went outside. 'Problem is,' he said, throwing her an oil skin jacket, 'where do we start looking?'

'Let's skirt part of the lake,' she said, donning the coat, a couple of sizes too big.

'This pig: the one you saw in your trance,' said Freddie, as they walked briskly along the east shore, 'did you notice its markings?'

'All I could think about was how to get back to the land of the living and to you.' She squeezed his hand.

There were not many people chancing the November outdoors that cold Sunday afternoon, but they did see one familiar face:

'Freddie Pearson!'

Freddie stopped dead in his tracks. He'd know that voice anywhere. He turned to see George Pym hurrying towards them, his cheeks the colour of his long plum scarf.

'Bless my soul! Freddie!'

'Hello, Mr Pym.'

'Fancy seeing you. On holiday, are you?'

'Ehm, in a way, yes. This is Sophie, a friend.'

George shook her firmly by the hand. 'Extraordinary, bumping into you like this. You didn't mention anything about a holiday. You're in a frightful hurry by the looks of things.'

'We are,' he said, edging to get away.

'Well, I won't keep you.' He gave a small cough. 'But before you go, tell me, do you happen to know The Black Dog Inn?'

'We've just come from there,' said Sophie.

'Really? Only the strangest thing happened to me the other night.'

Freddie and Sophie exchanged looks.

'Mr Pym?' said Freddie. 'Have you ever performed an exorcism?'

'An exorcism?' He thought for a moment. 'Well, no, now you mention it. Baptisms yes, funerals yes, weddings yes, exorcisms ...' He shook his head.

'We need your help,' urged Sophie.

'Urgently,' said Freddie.

'You want me to perform an exorcism?'

'Possibly. We'll explain as we go. '

'Go where?' He looked about him helplessly. 'I can't be away long, Sheila will be expecting me.'

'Please, help us,' implored Sophie. 'It's a matter of life and death.'

'We're looking for a ghost – a ghost on the run,' said Freddie.

His eyes twinkled. 'Nothing to do with The Black Dog Inn, by any chance?'

'Yes. Everything to do with it,' said Freddie. 'There's a pig on the loose. He belonged to my grandfather.'

'A pig?'

'A black pig. He was slaughtered, but now he's returned.'

'How on earth?'

'We had a séance – it materialised. We'll tell you on the way.'

Sophie touched his arm. 'He might harm the landlady, you see.'

'Oh, dear. That is bad. I was about to call on her too. Well, my dear, since you put it like that.' He drew up his coat collar. 'I think,' he said, as they set off, 'that it's a good idea to have some plan should we happen upon this nefarious beast.'

'What sort of plan?' asked Freddie.

'Tradition has it that if the devil enters a pig, it does so through very small apertures in the animal's forefeet. If you remove the hair in this area you can see a burnt, ring-like mark which gives the appearance of having been branded onto the foot. Does he have a name this pig?'

'Bellygod.'

'Very well. If Bellygod is possessed, and there is a strong possibility that he might be, let us assume for argument's sake that the evil spirit, or spirits entered through his forefeet. Working on the premise that the feet may also act as a line of exit, an exorcism might be effected through this same channel.'

'It's certainly worth a try,' said Freddie. 'You know this area, don't you? Can you suggest a route for us to take, Mr Pym?'

'We could follow this lakeshore.'

'And then?'

'A mile on from here and opposite the north end of *Belle Isle* is a footpath that leads to woodland. This eventually opens onto moorland before dropping down into *Far Sawry*. We could continue in that direction, if you like.'

'We'll be guided by you, but it's getting dark already and we didn't bring torches.'

'Never without one.' George, patting his side pocket.

After walking a quarter of a mile, Sophie stopped to remove a pebble from her shoe. 'Do you hear that church bell?' asked Freddie, as they waited for her. 'It's coming from over the other side of those trees, I think.'

'What time is it?' asked George.

Freddie glanced at his watch: 'Five o'clock.'

'Mm.' George thought for a moment. 'It could be the evensong bell, I suppose, or it is just possible that it may be a distress signal. If my memory serves me, it is coming from a small disused church, more a chapel really, a little further on. Now then, what's that sapient rhyme? "When the bell begins to toll, Lord have mercy upon thy soul." Yes, yes indeed! We must hurry.'

 fourteen

'You really think,' Sophie panted, after walking for a further five minutes, 'that it could be Doris ringing that thing?'

'If it is Doris, full marks to her, I say,' said George, striding ahead. 'During the Second World War, we clergyman were ordered to ring the parish church bell the moment we feared invasion. What better way of warning others of impending danger.'

'We'd better keep close,' Freddie warned, 'If Bellygod has followed her, he could be hiding in the bushes.

They picked their way down a narrow path that led to a small, overgrown churchyard. The church itself was overhung and dark. Sycamore and birch tangled with ash and yew and years of neglect had given rise to bramble and gorse. Saplings ate into the fabric of the building and had taken root in the eaves, crumbling the stone and stamping their own beauty, decadent and dire onto a place derelict and unremembered. The beaten blind arcading was cracked and only the arched entrance with its ornamental moldings remained in tact. They tramped on, through sodden grass, the tall brambles tearing at their clothes until finally they reached the church porch. Here, hymn books: damp darkened, covers curled, lay scattered on dusty shelves. Leaves, confetti crisp lay underfoot, and somewhere in the porch, a hedgehog stirred.

Freddie slowly turned the handle of the rust corroded door and they stepped inside, huddling together for warmth. George beamed his torch across the length of the nave. Six rows of boxed pews flanked a single aisle that was covered with rodent nibbled carpet. With the torchlight to guide them they made their way towards a torn, serge curtain. Slowly, cautiously, they drew it aside. In the middle of the floor, surrounded by half broken pews and old hassocks, stood Doris pulling on a bell rope. Her hair was dishevelled, her dress torn and her face running with sweat.

'Doris!' they chorused.

'Am I pleased to see you!' she wheezed, her fat arms shaking with effort.

'Are you all right?' asked Sophie going to her side.

'I've felt better.'

'Come and sit down.'

'You crazy?' she screeched. 'If I stop pulling this thing, that bleedin' pig will attack me.'

'But where is he?' Sophie looked nervously about her.

''E's out there somewhere, don't you worry. Look, will one of you gents take over before me arm falls off?'

'Of course. Allow me,' said George.

'No, no, allow *me*!' insisted Freddie.

'Oh, give it to me.' Sophie took the rope and began pulling while the men escorted Doris to a pew and sat on either side of her.

Freddie said, 'This is The Reverend Pym. He may be able to help us.'

'Pleased to meet you, your Reverend.' She took a handkerchief from the front of her dress and mopped her face.

'Would you like to tell us what happened,' cooed George, absent-mindedly patting her knee.

'Well, I've never run so fast in me life. Hadn't a clue where I was goin' mind, but when you've a ragin' pig on your tail, you don't 'ang about.'

'Quite so,' George removed his overcoat and placed it round her shoulders.

'So I run and I keep runnin': what else can I do?'

'You ran all this way with that bad back?' said Freddie, impressed.

'I was scared. You'll do anything when you're scared. As for me runnin': I won a cup for the ten thousand metres when I was in the fourth form.' Murmurs of approval.

'Come in 'andy that did. It's amazin' what you learn, even at school. Anyway, I come across this church and I remembered from somewhere that evil spirits don't like anyfink 'oly, so I make a dash for it, run inside and slam the door. Lot of good that done. Next thing, the bloody thing's inside wiv me, starin' me full in the face like it done earlier.'

'Before he chased you out of the inn?' prompted Freddie.

'That's right. Well, I hide behind this curtain, but 'e comes after me – stands there all quiverin' and bristly. Then I spot the bell rope. Well, I never rung a bell in me life. I look at it hangin' there, moth eaten and that, and I look at 'im and I think, what's the odds? So I pull it, and bugger me, it works!'

'It's a miracle it didn't come off in your hand. The rope looks rotten.' Freddie, wished he had brought his notebook with him.

'It stopped Belly whatsit in 'is tracks, anyway. Then 'e vanished – Poof!'

'Amazing!' said George.

'Yeh, but then, thinkin' I was safe, I stopped me ringin, didn't I? And 'e suddenly appeared again, snortin' and gruntin' and actin' all threatenin' like. So I went back to tollin' again and 'e vanished like before.' She pulled the jacket close, her expression thoughtful. 'Wonderful things is bells.'

'Indeed they are,' agreed George. 'Have you heard of *The Hallowed Bell*, Doris?'

'A pub, is it?'

'Not a pub, no. Years ago it was thought that church bells had the power to drive away devils and hence the term, "Ringing the Hallowed Bell." Bells were rung to help rid pestilence and storm as well as summoning people to worship, and also as a protection against fire.'

'Very interesting your Reverend. But shouldn't we be making a run for it?'

'If you are feeling up to it.' He turned to Freddie. 'I'll get Sophie. You keep Doris company until I return.'

George slid to the end of the pew, opened its little door

and took his first step. He stepped out onto what felt like a palpitating bolster: long, curved and firm. There was a grunt, a snort, then a howl, a bellow and a roar. Dropping his torch, he hurtled over the bolster and landed hard on his back. A wet, slobbering snout nuzzled his face. Something tugged and clawed at his neck. His clerical collar! He put his hand to his throat but his collar had gone, vanished. There were loud munching sounds in his left ear. He tried to get up but was pinned to the ground by firm pulsating flesh.

'Help somebody! Get him off me!' he screamed.

'I'm coming!' shouted Freddie. But found himself wedged between Doris and the pew.

'Freddie! Freddie! Where are you?' called Sophie, frantically feeling her way in the dark.

Doris, preparing to meet her maker, began singing *Jerusalem* at the top of her voice, while the bolster, not bargaining for the collar studs, started to choke.

'Excuse me,' boomed a male voice from the back of the church.

'Who's there?' shouted Freddie.

'It's Dave.'

Dave?

'Is Samuel there?'

'Who?'

'Samuel, my pig. He wanders in here sometimes. Likes the churchyard – plenty of berries, see.'

'We can't see anything,' Freddie yelled. 'We've lost our torch.'

'I've got one. Hang on.'

'Will someone get this animal off me,' moaned George.

'Come on Samuel,' called Dave, shining his torch on the two of them. 'Leave that poor man alone now, do.'

They all stared at the black pig, whose front feet were pinned firmly on George's chest.

'Samuel! Come on now.'

The pig pricked up his ears, gave a couple of resonant burps then trotted amiably to Dave's side.

'Good gracious!' exclaimed George, lifting himself onto his elbows and viewing the bolster for the first time. 'I had no idea he was so large.'

Sophie rushed over and helped George to his feet while Freddie, seeing Dave and his companion walk casually towards the church door, shouted, 'Stop! You can't walk out of here with someone else's pig.'

Dave turned. 'What do you mean, someone else's pig? He's my pig. I'll do what I want.'

'He is not your pig.'

'He is. So! I'd know my Samuel anywhere.'

'How would you know?' Freddie challenged.

'His front trotter.' Dave lifted the pig's front, right foot, and gave it a triumphant shake. 'It's white, see? That's his special marking: a white, right, front trotter. Now, if you don't mind, Samuel will be wanting his tea.'

'We do mind actually,' said Sophie, speaking up.

'Are you telling me I don't know my own pig, young lady?'

'What she's trying to tell you,' defended Freddie, 'is that there is some mistake. This pig, my pig, also has a white, right, front trotter. He belonged to my grandfather.'

Dave took off his glasses and blinked.

'And further more,' continued Freddie, 'I think I should warn you that this pig is highly dangerous.'

'Dangerous? Don't make me laugh!'

'He eats people. So there!'

'I've heard it all now. Samuel wouldn't harm a fly. Look at him.'

There was no answer to that. The pig looked adoringly up at Dave: his eyes soft, watery and slack.

George drew Freddie aside. 'Are you quite sure this is Bellygod?'

'Of course I'm sure. But do you think we should tell him?'

'I think we have no option.'

'Dave,' said Freddie, walking over to him.

'What now?' The pig was lying on his back, having his tummy scratched.

'We think you ought to know something.'

'What?'

'This pig. The pig you think is your pig, is – well, it's dead.'

'Dead?'

'Yes, dead.'

'You nuts or something? Does he look dead?'

'Now, now,' placated George, 'Let's not raise our voices. Remember where we are. What Freddie is trying to say, young man, is that our pig, the pig we think is ours ...'

'Know is ours, Mr Pym,' corrected Freddie.

'Know is ours, was slaughtered some years back and has now returned to haunt us. Try and be sensible, Dave. We are only thinking of your safety. You understand what I am saying?'

Dave gawped. 'You're weird – you know that? The lot of you's weird.' He pointed at George. 'And you call yourself a man of God? Come on, Samuel.'

The pig stood up, and without the merest grunt of protest, trotted obediently and peacefully out of the west door with Dave in tow.

'Wait!' Freddie yelled, running after him. 'Stop! You can't do this. Come back! Do you hear? Come back now!'

'Let him go,' said Doris, unusually mollified.

Freddie stared first at her and then at George, who eyed him sheepishly. 'Are you thinking what I think you're thinking?'

They stayed silent.

He turned to Sophie. 'Well, what do you think?'

She shrugged. 'Maybe Dave possesses the magic touch. Who knows? It is extraordinary.'

'Extraordinary!' echoed George, who doubted that his exorcism would have proved anywhere near as effective.

'And if Dave really believes that Bellygod is Samuel –' continued Sophie.

'And we did try to convince him that he wasn't,' contributed George.

'Then who's to know and who's to say?' finished Doris, her religious phase now at an end. 'The fact is we're rid of 'im, and if Dave wants 'im then let 'im have 'im. Let's just be grateful for this lucky intervention and get out of 'ere before 'im upstairs,' raising her eyes heavenwards, 'decides different.'

Ø Ø

Doris produced a large bottle of brandy from one of the bar shelves. 'Come on, Sophie girl, warm yourself on this. You look all in.' Then turning to George, 'You'll have a nip, Your Reverend?'

'Thank you, but I must get back to my wife – she'll be wondering where on earth I've got to.' He stood warming his hands by the fire. 'This has been the most extraordinary experience. I don't think I shall ever be quite the same again.'

Doris tossed back her head and laughed, her belly heaving with delight. 'It's put me right off pork, I can tell you. But I'll say one thing,' casting her eye around the room, 'Them ghosts do tidy up after themselves.'

'Yes,' agreed Freddie. 'It's a miracle really, the way everything's back in place.'

'And no broken glass either,' marvelled Sophie. 'The spring clean must have happened while we were out searching for Doris. I wonder who was responsible for that?' She went over to George and kissed his cheek. 'Thank you Mr Pym for all you've done – leading us to Doris and bringing us home safe and sound.'

'A pleasure, my dear. Although, I didn't do my job, or let's say, I didn't finish my job, did I?'

'What do you mean?'

'I didn't exorcise Bellygod.'

'Next best thing though.' Doris nudged him in the ribs. 'Belly whatsit's evil spirit departed, just like you said it would – through 'is feet. 'E walked out that church door, sweet as pie.'

'So he did,' laughed George, turning to leave.

'Thanks so much, Mr Pym.' Freddie shook him warmly by the hand and walked with him to the door.

'Where's Harold?' asked Sophie, after he'd gone, guiltily aware that she had forgotten all about him.

''Es probably taken 'imself off to the cinema,' said Doris, pouring herself another brandy. 'Harold's never 'ad a stomach for anythink stronger than beer.' She opened the till and began counting the small change.

'Ah, well,' sighed Freddie, who could think of nothing he would like better than to be on his own with Sophie. 'I expect he'll turn up soon.' And then putting his arm around her, 'We'll be in our room if you need us.'

Doris shut the till with a resounding bang. 'You can 'ave 'im,' she said.

'What?'

'Sir Egbert. Take 'im.'

He and Sophie exchanged looks. 'Doris, do you mean that, really?'

'I mean it, all right. Who's to say that 'e wasn't responsible for that pig appearin'? I wouldn't put it passed the old codger. Probably resurrected 'im from 'is old estate.' She flooded a dish with peanuts. 'We're better off without him, 'es a miserable old sod.'

Sophie tried to explain that Bellygod had nothing to do with Sir Egbert that it was she who had raised the pig's spirit, but Doris wouldn't listen, her mind was made up. Relief at being home safe and sound had mollified her feelings towards Sophie. She was a good girl, a credit to her mother. 'Mind you,' she went on, a note of reverence entering her voice, 'I did like the other one. Now he 'ad class. Pity 'es gone. Yes, I liked 'im.' She flung a couple of dirty beer glasses into a bowl of suddy water. 'I'm sure we could have done a nice bit of business there, Thomas and me. Shame.'

Freddie, keen to clinch the deal said, 'This is a definite yes, Doris?'

She nodded, took a cloth and wiped the bar. 'Get 'im out of 'ere quick though. I don't want 'im 'angin' around a minute longer than necessary. Now, if you'll excuse me, folks.'

She turned to serve a customer. 'What'll it be, love?'

fifteen

Adelina and Thomas sat staring at an eight-foot hedge.

'Try again, Thomas.'

He stood up, placed his right leg three feet in front of his left, his right arm forty degrees off the vertical. Next he bent his right leg, elevated for two feet, coasted for three, before sinking back to the ground. 'It is no good,' he said testily. 'There is not enough room for lift off.'

'Try again, do.'

'I wish you would stop saying that, Adelina,' he returned sulkily, and together they sat on in moody silence.

'Hopeless,' he said eventually. 'How long have we been sitting here, like stuffed dummies?'

'You arrived from Windermere yesterday evening around dusk.'

'Yes, well, judging by the sun's position, it must be approximately nine o'clock in the morning now. So say sixteen hours, sixteen hours we have been incarcerated in this place.'

'And *I* have been here a good deal longer,' she reminded him gently.

'If I could just gain enough height to scale this damnable hedge, I could perhaps get us some help. I do not understand why I cannot do it. Gliding has always been my forte.'

'Indeed it has.' A shadow of a smile.

'I must say, you remain surprisingly calm,' Thomas remarked irritably. 'Your antennae have been working overtime. I think.' He peered at her closely. 'You have been part puppeteer in all this caper. Am I right?'

Silence.

'That business with the pig, for instance.'

'Ah, yes. Ignatius.'

'Ignatius?'

'The pig.'

'You mean Bellygod, surely?'

'No, I mean Ignatius. It was vital that Sophie and Freddie should think it was Bellygod. If they had thought, if they had known it was gentle Ignatius who would not harm a fly, let alone Doris, they would not have given such convincing performances.'

'That was extremely devious of you, Adelina,' said Thomas, ruffled by this revelation. 'I would not have thought you had it in you.'

'No,' she replied simply, 'I do not suppose you would.'

'I really wish you had made your presence known to us,' he grumbled. 'Freddie and Sophie were working in the dark. And so was I, come to think of it.'

'It was essential to get things moving, Thomas.'

'But I was there. I was helping,' he put in quickly.

'Of course you were there, but there were problems – you saw that. Doris needed a scare: something to bring the woman to her senses.'

He grunted. 'If Ignatius is as gentle as you say, why did he act in that ferocious manner?'

'Because I told him to. He acted on my instructions. Anyway, he was not ferocious for long. He left the church quiet as a lamb.'

'You exert considerable influence over this pig. I do not remember this Ignatius.'

'That is because I did not tell you about him and Egbert hated pigs except for meat, so I did not tell him either.'

'From the estate, was he, this animal?'

'Yes. He was such an endearing creature with quite a little personality. I used to visit the pigs regularly and grew particularly fond of Ignatius. I watched him grow, mature. When the time came for him to be slaughtered, I stole into his stye late one night, put a rope round his neck and led him to Chinkton Manor Woods. There was plenty of food for him there: berries, roots and so forth. I visited him most days, then one day he did not answer my call. I searched and searched but never found him. He was probably hunted and killed; provided a meal for some hungry family – who knows what happened. I was very sad for a while.'

'So, you did a little re-casting, did you?'

'I did what I thought necessary.'

'Cunning.'

'That makes two of us then.'

Thomas stroked her cheek, kissed her mouth. 'Here we sit,' he murmured, 'like two angels with our wings clipped. I have let you down badly. I should have taught you to glide – made you self reliant, and then perhaps, you could have rescued me.'

'You came, and that is what matters,' she said, resting her head on his shoulder.

'Your eau de Cologne touched me with its sharpness – held a mirror to my soul.'

Adelina giggled as she played with his waistcoat buttons. 'Save the purple prose for your young ghost friend, my dear.'

He drew back. 'What young ghost friend?'

'That pretty, lost soul who waited for you outside the library window. You deserted me, for her. You never gave me that gliding lesson and look what has happened as a result.'

'She meant nothing to me, believe me.'

'That is what they all say.' Then after a moment: 'Thomas?'

'Mm?'

'Will you do me a favour?'

'That depends.'

'Employ Maurice. Let him work with you at The Black Dog Inn.'

'Good heavens!' Thomas stared in surprise. 'In what capacity?'

'As actor manager. He knows a good deal about the

theatre and could be a great asset to you.'

He thought for a moment. 'Mm. Yes, someone like Maurice might do very well – very well indeed. Why, thank you Adelina. I think it an excellent idea.'

'You will take him on?'

'If Doris approves. Yes, I think I will. She wanted to keep two ghosts – well now she can have them! Wonderful! This could be the answer to our problems. I will get back to her at once. And then if I have the all clear, I will make a flying visit to see Maurice.' His face dropped. 'That is, if and when we ever get out of this place.'

'Oh, thank you, Thomas,' she said, rising to her feet and holding out her hand. 'That makes me feel a whole lot better. Come on.'

'What do you mean, come on, come on where?'

'Take my hand.'

'What for?'

'Do as I ask.'

'My God!' he said, taking hold of her fingers, 'You are glowing like a copper kettle.' He felt a tug at his heels, glanced at his feet and was dismayed to find that he had lifted a couple of feet off the ground. Then came another tug, harder this time and Thomas rose higher. Adelina's skirts swirled round his feet as she whipped into the air alongside him. She squeezed his hand and they rose higher still. Soundlessly, they coasted the hedges: hovered, drifted, hovered some more then glided mellifluously along the length of the maze, leaving behind them a plethora of thick green yew.

'I must say, Adelina,' remarked Thomas, as they scaled the vegetable garden, 'your navigational skills have certainly improved, not to mention your gliding. What has happened?'

'I have no idea.' She laughed, rather prettily, he thought, and letting go his hand, dropped in height and performed a little pirouette immediately beneath the soles of his shoes.

'Yes, very good Adelina – most impressive,' he said,

following in her wake, 'But I must think about making tracks: must head off to Windermere, if I am to put in my offer about your son.' He hesitated. 'Where will you go? Back to the curate's?'

'Oh no, not now.' She attempted a mid-air curtsey, 'I will return to the manor now.'

'Do you think that is wise, Adelina?'

'I can glide, as you see, so I will not break anything. I am no longer a risk to their property. Besides, I must go home, be there to welcome Egbert. He will be back any time.' Another pirouette.

Thomas treaded the air, vigorously trying to keep level with her. 'Are there messages you would like me to relay when I return to Windermere?'

'Yes. Tell Egbert that I expect him soon. That I long to see him again.'

'Very well,' he replied tartly.

'And say nothing about the pig.'

'No.'

'And be sure to ask Doris about Maurice.'

'Of course.'

She spun round to face him. 'Then this is goodbye Thomas, and thank you.'

'Do I get a farewell kiss, Adelina?'

She proffered her cheek but he sought her mouth, kissing it eagerly. She excited him more than ever. No longer dependent on him, ever accessible, easy to please – Adelina had now become an enigma, a little remote: a tantalizing conundrum. Yes, he liked that.

'I could delay Windermere for another half hour or so,' he said, treading the air faster. 'The astral airways are fairly clear this time of day.' He held her tight, and the two of them spun, dipped and soared, like massive birds in the morning sky.

'You must go now,' she said eventually, pulling away and adjusting her mob cap.

'Shall I visit you at the manor?'

'I do not know that Sir Egbert would want that. But we shall see.'

He smiled, bowed and left her then: sailing over the orchard, the rose garden, the lawn, away over the fields to the distant low hills, until he was no more than a black speck on the horizon.

It was now Adelina's turn. Her descent was perfect: her landing smooth and effortless as her long toes touched down on the lawn. Gliding with expert grace towards the manor, she ascended the terrace steps passing Lady Wilham on her way out with the dogs. For Brill and Tope, seeing their old friend again was like retrieving an old, bone and they greeted Adelina with tails wagging. Lady Wilham hesitated, turned, a puzzled look on her face then shrugging her shoulders, called the dogs to heel before setting off across the grass for her morning walk.

Adelina entered the hall and glided towards the library. The few remaining ornaments, those she had not broken, had been removed but she supposed that was to be expected. It felt so good to be back among the warm smell of books, the open fire, the sweet aroma of apple wood. Nothing much had changed. She sat in her chair to the right of the fireplace and thought about the messages she must send. There was Ignatius to thank for the magnificent part he had played. For him she would create an illusion of roots, barley meal, brewer's grains and beans. Dave would be reunited with his own pig and be none the wiser. And Freddie and Sophie? They deserved something special. She would have to think about them. Last on her agenda, was Simon. Adelina squirmed. Would he, could he find it in his heart to forgive her? Settling deep into her chair and luxuriating in her new found success, she pondered hard and long on what she should do to make amends.

∅ ∅

Freddie was on edge. Playing sardines with an eighteenth

century ghost was not his idea of fun.

'Come in, come in!' urged Egbert, flinging open the airing cupboard door. 'We will not be disturbed in here.'

'If it's all the same to you,' said Sophie, seeing the look on Freddie's face, 'we'll stand outside. It is rather warm in there.'

'Just as you wish.' Egbert leaned despondently against the water tank.

Freddie said, 'We were so worried when you faded away from the séance; we thought that we would never see you again.'

'It was awful! I could not perpetuate my luminosity another second. And Thomas does so enjoy the sound of his own voice. Anyway, here I am, not at my brilliant best, I admit, but here anyway. So, tell me your news.'

'And wonderful news, Sir Egbert! You are free to leave. We have the say so from old Doris.'

'Yes, I know that. Thomas told me.'

'You've seen Thomas – he's back?'

He nodded resignedly. 'Oh, yes, he is back. He left the séance to rescue my wife; but of course, you know that. What you may not know, is that she was stuck, poor woman. And Thomas too, when he went to rescue her; they were both stuck in Chinkton Manor Maze.' He chuckled and then seeing their look of concern, 'They got out eventually though, and Adelina, bless her heart, has reinstated herself at the manor.'

'She's been in touch with you?' Freddie.

He nodded and then in a low voice, 'But what I would like to know and what Thomas would not tell me, is what finally persuaded Doris to change her mind.'

'Didn't he tell you about the pig?' Sophie.

'Oh pigs! I hate 'em,' said Egbert, throwing himself against the water tank. 'We kept 'em on our farm. Adelina wanted one as a pet but I forbade it. Imagine! A pig as a pet. Anyway, what about this pig?'

'He's a relation of Freddie's.'

'Hang on, Sophie. He's not a relation of mine. You see, Sir

Egbert, Bellygod, this pig, lived on my grandfather's farm. One day he escaped from his sty, attacked and ate him.'

'Dear me. A vicious beast then.'

'This one was. Anyway, by sheer bad luck, it materialised at the séance. Sophie raised the beast by accident. She's an animal psychic, you see,' Freddie squeezed her hand. 'And a very talented one too.'

'Well, anyway,' continued Sophie, feeling herself blush, 'Bellygod then chased Doris all the way to an old disused church where the pig was hiding in wait.'

Egbert sat down on a pile of towels.

'Then,' went on Freddie, 'someone called Dave walked into the church and took him away. He said that the pig belonged to him. But the strange thing was that the moment Bellygod saw Dave, he changed and became sweet as pie. But now, Doris wants you out of here fast. She insists that Sophie had nothing to do with the manifestation of Bellygod.'

'She thinks you did it, Sir Egbert.' Sophie stared at her feet, shame faced. 'Even though I insisted that you didn't.'

'But I would not do such a thing. Not even to Doris. Oh, dear, that quite distresses me.'

'She thinks it was out of malice and revenge, you see.'

'Oh dear, oh dear,' now wringing his hands. 'I just hope my son, Maurice can cope with that woman, I really do.'

'Maurice, your son – coming here?' Sophie's eyebrows shot up in amazement.

'He plans to join forces with Thomas. The sooner I leave and make way for him, the better. Yes.' And he stared forlornly at one of Harold's shirts, awaiting the iron. 'I should like to have seen Maurice before I go, you know. It is a great sadness to me that we never got on.'

'Perhaps you will meet him, Sir Egbert.' Sophie longed to put her arms around him.

'Perhaps.' He sighed and the water tank gurgled as though in sympathy. 'Well, we had better get on.'

'Right,' said Sophie.

'Ready,' said Freddie.

Egbert rose to his feet. 'Now then, I had best put you in the picture. If, and only if I can draw on enough cosmic energy,' now venturing from the airing cupboard and into the bathroom, 'a white pool of light will appear in front of me. You must both direct me into that light. Once I enter the radiant zone, you are to say the words, "We release you, Egbert!" It is important that you concentrate, as that will empower me further.'

'Will we ever see you again?' asked Sophie, close to tears.

'So long as you keep your psychic powers alive then I do not see why not.' He held out his arms and Freddie took a step backwards. 'Thank you both for everything,' he said, 'I could not have managed without your help and enormous support.'

It was at that moment an ear-splintering scream sent Sophie and Freddie running onto the landing. Doris was reeling at the top of the stairs, clutching her sides as though in pain.

'What is it Doris?' Freddie ran to her side.

'What is it? Harold's gone, that's what! Packed a couple of shirts, 'is underpants and 'is one good suit and cleared awf.'

'But why would he do that?'

'Frightened fartless, I expect. And who can blame him?' Her eyes were red with black mascara lining her cheeks. 'E's got a lot to answer for that ghost of yours – raising Bellygod like 'e done and then taking my Harold.'

'You mustn't keep blaming Sir Egbert,' said Sophie. 'He had nothing to do with raising Bellygod. I told you that before.'

But Doris wasn't listening. 'I 'ad it all planned out,' she sniffed. 'We'd save a bit then retire to the Costa Brava. We never 'ad much, you know; just eked out a living like everyone else.'

'Come down to the bar,' said Freddie, taking her arm and leading her tottering down the wooden stairs. 'Come on, and I'll fix you a brandy to steady your nerves.' Halfway down she turned. 'I want that Egbert out of 'ere double quick, do I make myself clear? So you do what you 'ave to do soon as you can. Maybe Harold will come 'ome once that monster's gone.' She continued her rocky course, one hand clutching the banisters the other, Freddie's arm.

'This is all very distressing,' said Egbert, popping his head round the bathroom door.

'Shall I say the words, Sir Egbert? Can we manage with just me?' asked Sophie, her hands shaking.

'I doubt that either of you can shift me now. This recent foray – this incursion of my soul has affected my vibrations more than ever.'

'But Egbert, you mustn't allow Doris to get to you like this. She's just a stupid insensitive woman, who will stop at nothing to get her own way.'

'I feel too much, my dear, that is the trouble. I become easily aggrieved.' He shook his head hovering over the radiator.

'You must try to remain positive, Sir Egbert.'

'Well, if you say so. We may as well have a go now, I suppose. We have nothing to lose.' And he wondered out onto the landing. 'Are we alone?'

Sophie walked the length of the corridor. Every room was shut.

'We'd better be quick,' she said.

'I am ready.'

He moved to the top of the stairs, stood very still and closed his eyes. The clock on the landing ticked away and downstairs there was the usual chatter and laughter as the bar began to fill. Then just when Sophie thought nothing was going to happen, three feet ahead of them, directly over a threadbare patch of carpet, there appeared a grimy yellow circle of light.

Egbert groaned. 'There! Just l … l … look at that sickly w … wattage. I c … cannot do anything w … with th … th … that.'

'What's the matter with your speech? It's gone all funny again,' said Sophie. 'And your voice is faint, just like it was at the séance.'

'I am b … b … blocked. My l … light transmission is b … b … below p … par. And there is something else b … b bothering me but I am not sure wh … what it is.'

'I see. Well, look. Why don't you have a rest and a quiet think. We can try again later.'

Egbert nodded, gave Sophie a desultory wave, and retired once more to the airing cupboard. He had reached an all time low. It had not taken them long to replace him and it was time to face up to the fact that he was now a matter of no import – a nullity. It was Thomas: had always been Thomas who possessed the aplomb, the artistic flare and that wretched thing called sex appeal. And it was good, he supposed that the fellow had volunteered to take his place. He was grateful – he really was. It was just that he felt he had been thrown onto the spiritual scrap heap, so to speak. Despite hating it up here, there was still a niggling sense of loss at the thought of leaving The Black Dog Inn. Ambivalent feelings were always so wretchedly confusing and disorientating. Hurt ego that was what it was. He had grown accustomed to grumbling, grown accustomed to the pain and discomfort of his years spent up here. Perhaps, in the end though, unwelcome exposure was preferable to none at all. He had at least served some purpose, provided entertainment of sorts. Alas, what now? What would his role be now? How would he occupy his time at the manor? There was no such thing as, The Family Ghost anymore – Adelina had seen to that.

The airing cupboard; normally so warm, so comforting and secure, felt suddenly chilly, unwelcoming and strange, as though it were pushing him out – evicting him, almost. He tried settling next to a pile of blankets, but they prickled his neck and made it sore. Restless and sad, he glided once more onto the landing. But here too it was unusually cold. As he hovered, uncertain as to what he should do, where he should go, he sensed a presence – a familiar presence at that. Not Adelina, not Thomas and yet he felt sure it was a spirit he had once known well. Slowly, very slowly he turned his head and there, clear as day, a few feet in front of him, encircled by white light, his brown hair tied back with a velvet ribbon, stood his son.

'Hello, Father.'

'Maurice!'

They hovered, staring at one another. Neither spoke.

'I cannot believe my eyes.' Egbert said, at last.

'I know. Mother says you have been unhappy here. I am sorry.'

'We are a family of refugees, Maurice.' He broke off. 'But this is wonderful! I thought I should never see you again.' He hugged him then and together they coasted the landing. 'So, you have come to join Thomas with his jolly bag of tricks, have you?'

'You do not approve, Father. I know, there is no need to say any more.'

'The acting profession was not the career I had mapped out for you, true. But I now see that I was wrong to impose my will.'

Maurice opened his eyes in surprise.

'To reach our higher planes,' Egbert went on, 'we must cultivate our more positive attributes. I daresay you know what you are doing. And I hope that you are not too old to accept my blessing.'

'You really do not mind, Father?'

'Mind? My dear boy, after everything that we have been through – you, your mother and I, how can I possibly mind?'

Maurice shook him warmly by the hand while Egbert held back the tears. What a pleasure it was to see his son happy and smiling, instead of glowering, peevish and sulky. Ah, yes. This was a good feeling. To be re-united with your son: to bury past differences. Yes, Egbert felt very much better now.

'Your light, Father,' said Maurice, shading his eyes, 'It is brighter.'

'No – really?'

'I do not think I have ever seen another ghost as brilliantly lit as you. And your voice is stronger too; without a stutter.'

'Brilliant, am I? No stutter? That is good news.' He glanced down at his brown velvet costume. It gleamed, shimmered almost. 'This is great news,' he said. 'With this amount of wattage, I can now move under my own steam, and without the help of Sophie or Freddie too. Before you came, Maurice, the glow I emitted was scarcely a glow at all. I projected a very feeble light, so weak – so useless – it did nothing at all.'

'Not anymore though.'

'Not anymore.' He grasped his son by the hand. 'You have acted like a generator, Maurice. I cannot thank you enough.'

'You have thanked me.'

'How so?'

'You have liberated me and as a result, you have liberated yourself. Do you realise, Father, that this is the first time that you have ever given me your approval – your blessing. Your love and good opinion matter to me. Now it seems I have both.'

Sir Egbert looked deeply into his son's eyes. 'I have always loved you, make no mistake but perhaps, well perhaps I did not express it too well.'

'Who is to say what frees us in the end? It may be a word, a kindness, an action, or love. We have changed – all of us – moved on. You, Mother, Thomas, and me. Even Doris will be different now.'

'You will come and visit us, Maurice?' said Egbert, hugging him.

'Of course I will.'

'Oh, now then, I almost forgot. I must let Sophie and Freddie know I am leaving. After all they have done for me.'

'There is not time for that, Father. You must go now, while things are quiet and while you have your glow. They will understand.'

'Do you think? It does seem so ungracious to leave with-out saying my farewells.' And after a moment's pause, 'Oh, very well.' He took hold of Maurice's hand. 'I hope you will be happier up here than I was. Oh, dear, that was not very tactful, was it? But, you know what I mean. I am certain in any case, that your love of the theatre will sustain you – it has done so in the past. Come and see us soon.'

'I promise to come and see you and Mother happily reunited back at the manor.'

Egbert raised his hand in a salute and vanished, leaving Maurice to cope with feelings about his father that he did not yet fully understand.

Ten minutes later Maurice and Thomas were discussing plans.

'Tomorrow,' announced Thomas, 'I will introduce you to Doris. She knows you are joining us. At present she is too unstable to speak to anyone. Her husband has recently left her and the woman is quite hysterical. She will get over it.' Thomas looked at him narrowly. 'Has your dear father left the premises?'

'Yes, he has gone.' What had taken place between them both was far too precious to share, especially with the likes of Thomas.

'Good, good. My plan helped no end, I am glad to say. Well, I daresay he will telegraph to thank me in due course. Freddie and the girl released him, did they?' And without waiting for a reply, 'Excellent, excellent. He was quite unsuited to this climate, you know. We have done him a great favour, taking his place. And now,' he pro-claimed, pacing up and down the corridor, 'we start afresh. A new epoch.' Maurice fell into step. 'I intend,' continued Thomas, 'to give the punters great entertain-ment. Conjuring tricks, cabarets, all that sort of thing.'

Maurice started. 'Conjuring tricks? Cabarets?'

'You look surprised.'

'What sort of conjuring tricks?'

'Apports, asports, that kind of thing.'

'Asports?' This was heretical.

'Yes, you know, the opposite of apports – objects that disappear from view. Whereas an apport is the manifestation of an object from out of thin air.'

'Yes, yes, I am well aware of what they are.' Such mention was a stern reminder of his past behaviour.

'So then, imagine how thrilled the lady members of our audience will be to receive free gifts from the spirit world. They are all the rage nowadays – free gifts. Then of course, we will produce materialisations, run competitions, maybe hold a lottery — Doris could organise that.'

'But ...'

'Yes?'

'What about Shakespeare?'

'What about him?'

'I thought we were planning to perform Shakespeare and scenes from Dryden – perhaps a little Congreve, Sheridan and Goldsmith. We could recite Wordsworth. The locals would enjoy listening to poems by their local hero, William Wordsworth.'

'But my dear boy,' said Thomas, masking his irritation, 'it has all been done before. You come from a theatre steeped in classical drama. What makes us so special is that we are unique. Just stop and think for a moment. How many people have attended a concert organised by ghosts? How many mortals have even seen a ghost let alone been entertained by one?' He flung his arms wide. 'We the dead shall entertain the living! We shall employ ghosts from the surrounding country houses. There is no end to our scope. The Black Dog Inn will be famous nationwide!'

'But ...'

'Yes?'

'I had this idea, you see,' Maurice stumbled, uncomfortably aware that his words were falling on deaf ears, 'that we would, as you suggested, engage ghosts from the surrounding country houses, yes, but perform plays, not variety acts.' His mouth twitched anxiously.

'Yes, I do see, I absolutely see,' he placated.

'I thought that you and I would be actor managers, following in the tradition of Colley Cibber. You remember Colley Cibber, the manager of Drury Lane?'

'Yes, yes, he and David Garrick and the rest of them. And I daresay,' Thomas went on hurriedly, 'that one day we will do something along those lines. But we must move with the times, Maurice. *We* need to be commercial – bums on seats and all that. The public wants to lock on to anything and everything that is new, different, and exciting. We must bear in mind the type of audience with whom we are dealing; not forgetting Doris, who, bless her heart, has probably never heard of Sheridan and judging from some of her customers, neither have they.' He took Maurice firmly by the arm. 'Cheer up. We will act the Bard, maybe sooner than you think, but we must test the water first. Rome was not built in a day. Now,' he said, chivvying him along the landing. 'Let me show you to your room.'

And with that, Thomas, firm but pleasant, ushered Maurice towards the recently vacated airing cupboard.

sixteen

'Well, Simon,' said George, as they sat sipping sherry in the rectory study, 'How do you feel?'

Simon caught his breath. 'Feel? What about?'

'My dear chap, your baptism by fire; taking charge of the parish in my absence, that's what about.'

He steeled himself for the worst. 'It's been er, interesting.'

'Mm.' George examined his glass as though looking for chips. 'The burial of ashes go off all right, did it?'

He knows, thought Simon, gazing despondently through the study window. 'Yes,' he said, 'the burial of ashes went well. But I expect Charles Neville has told you everything.'

'Charles has told me as much as he knows. Biscuit?'

Simon shook his head. He wished George would get to the point, stop playing games and put him out of his misery.

'You haven't found it easy here, have you Simon?' George re-settled himself in his chair.

'Well I ...'

'Coping with a parish, handling different people. There is an awful lot to learn in the ministry. It takes time; I understand that.'

'Do you?' Simon felt sick.

'Yes, I do. I was a young curate once, you know. I think that under the circumstances you coped admirably.'

Had he heard right. 'But surely you're –'

'Angry?' George shook his head. '"To err is human, to forgive divine." In any case you found the urn in time and that's the main thing.'

'Thank you for being so understanding,' he said, breathing more easily.

'There is one other thing.'

'Yes?' He was not out of the wood then.

George ambled over to his desk and sifted through some papers. 'I've received a letter from Lawrence Peacock. He wanted to tell me – now where did I put it? Ah, found it.' He waved a white, oblong envelope. 'He wanted to tell me how pleased he was with the way you conducted the service. He has enclosed a letter for you as well. Read it at your leisure,' he said, handing it to him.

'No, no – I'll read it now.' May as well face the music. There was bound to be more to all this than just thanks.

'Dear Mr Guest,' he read. 'First of all I would like to express my gratitude for the manner in which you took my dear wife's service of committal. It was a most moving ceremony, conducted with the utmost respect and sincerity. She would, I am sure, have appreciated the artistry and finesse with which you handled the occasion.

'On a different note: I have received a letter from the Biddling-

ton Police Constabulary, who have informed me of the unfortunate circumstances surrounding the temporary misplacement,
or as they termed it, theft of my late wife's ashes. They want to
know if I wish to press charges against your great aunt. Let me
put your mind at rest and assure you Mr Guest that I have no
intention of doing so. The fortitude with which you carried out
your ecclesiastical duties whilst stressed with the responsibility
of tending a relative of unsound mind, was, to say the least,
commendable. I apologise for my curtness towards you and hope
that should we meet in the future, we may put that little bit of
unpleasant misunderstanding behind us. Should you feel in
need of further support with regard to your aunt's ongoing
condition, I can recommend a first class psycho-therapist who
may be able to help. Again, please accept my thanks. Yours truly,
Lawrence Peacock. P.S. I have taken the liberty of placing your
Great Aunt Adelina on our parish church prayer list.'

This was an amazing piece of good luck. Simon, hands
shaking, returned the letter to its envelope aware that
George was staring at him.

'And how is your great aunt, Simon?' George had returned to his chair and was watching him.

He startled. 'Oh, up and down, you know. Mustn't complain.'

'Is she still staying with you?'

'Most definitely not. No.'

'I'm sorry to hear that you had this unfortunate business
to cope with on top of your parish duties. Relatives can be
very trying.'

'Oh well – all par for the course. How eh, how did you
know about my great aunt?'

'Charles Neville. He told me.'

Of course, the police must have mentioned her when
they rang him to check Simon's identity.

George said, 'This aunt of yours -'

'Great aunt.'

'Great aunt. I would like to meet her.'

'Would you?'

'Any chance?'

'Ah, difficult.'

'Perhaps in church one Sunday?'

'Never goes, I'm afraid. Firm atheist.'

'I see. Well, in that case, bring her for tea.'

'If she comes to stay again. Which she won't,' he added hurriedly. 'Well, not for a bit anyhow. She is very elusive, my great aunt. I've no idea where she is at present, absolutely no idea.'

'I see.'

Did Simon detect a twinkle? Well, it was his turn now. 'How was your holiday, George? Enjoyed it, did you?'

'Very much – a most enlightening experience; and I bumped into Freddie and his girlfriend Sophie, while we were there. Isn't that an extraordinary coincidence?'

'Yes,' said Simon, reddening, 'Freddie told me they were going to The Lake District.'

George eyed him sharply. 'Did he say why?'

He hesitated. Should he confide in George? Tell him the truth about Adelina? In a split second's decision, he opted against it. Old Lawrence Peacock had vindicated him; he'd best not push his luck. George would probably think he was barmy anyway, and yet he had the strangest feeling that the rector knew more than he was letting on – much more.

'Simon?' said George after a moment's pause.

'Yes?'

'Do you believe in an after life?'

'An after life? Yes, I think so.'

'You don't harbour doubts?'

'Maybe – sometimes. But it's healthy to doubt. It keeps the old brain working.' He eyed George closely. A new peace had settled on him since his return: a spiritual quality that was strikingly different.

'Now, Simon,' the rector continued, subject changed, 'you are not to worry about that incident with the urn. You offered solace to the bereaved and that is what matters. Our job lies in ministering, so let us forget the whole matter.'

'I may stay on as curate then?'

'My dear chap, how would I cope without you? I can ill afford to lose a man of your accomplishments.'

'Accomplishments? I wasn't aware I had any.'

'You take the church services far better than I do. Your voice carries well and you have an expressive delivery. Added to which you are a good parish visitor and friendly, and that is what people want and welcome in a village such as ours. And don't worry about Charles. Our churchwarden can be over zealous at times and quick to condemn. But as I am the rector, I hold pride of place and in my book, you stay. Now, you'll have that other sherry?'

'Thank you George.' Simon beamed. 'I think I will.'

'Seen anything of Liz Graham lately?' he asked, topping up their glasses.

'How lately do you mean?' returned Simon, surprised by the question.

'Since I went away. Only earlier this morning I bumped into her next door neighbour.'

'Gerald?'

'Gerald, yes. He was in the village shop, and we struck up a conversation.'

'You were honoured. He hardly says two words to me.'

'Really? Well, Gerald told me that Liz was thinking of moving back to London.'

'Well, that's city types for you.' He could hear the hard note in his voice and felt the ache in his heart. 'These people, they yearn for country life, the quintessential village green and all that stuff, but once they get it, they can't wait to return to city life.' This meeting had suddenly turned sour.

'Are you all right Simon?'

'I'm fine.' Too jovial now.

'You might pay her a visit on your way home,' he said,

gently.

'Me?' Simon's stomach lurched. 'Why me? I mean, she's not ill or anything is she?'

'No, not ill, a little down perhaps.'

'Why would Liz be down?'

'I have no idea, Simon. But Gerald seemed to think she was down in the mouth about something. And as priests it is our duty to keep a friendly eye on our flock.'

'But ...'

'Good heavens is that the time?' George glanced at the mantelpiece clock, 'I have to prepare for the vestry meeting this evening. You're coming?'

He nodded as George took his empty glass and placed it on the side-board. 'So you'll do that, will you?'

'Do what?'

'Call on Liz. Only it saves me.'

'Well I ...'

'Good. That's settled then.'

Ø Ø

The first thing Simon saw when he let himself in, was Adelina. She was sitting on the bottom of his stairs admiring her feet.

He closed his front door very slowly, very deliberately. He knew, seeing her there what he must do – it was just a case of when and in what order. Should he pack his suitcase before, or after lunch?

'Don't tell me,' he said his voice empty of emotion. 'Let me guess. You've decided to move in here with Egbert.'

'Silly boy!'

He flung his coat on the stairs. 'Nothing surprises me anymore.'

She shrugged. 'You have not asked me how I am.'

'How are you?' He'd eat, then pack.

'I am very well, thank you, Simon. Egbert and I are together again.'

'That's nice.' He longed to lie down. Sleep and sleep.

'Freddie and Sophie back, are they?'

'They are.' She floated to his side, neatly avoiding a porcelain vase on a stand – a recent acquisition from a boot sale.

'Well missed, Adelina. Your gliding's improved, I see.'

'I taught myself.'

'Thank God for that.'

'Poor Simon. You are in love.'

'Am I?' He supposed he was. He didn't know any more.

'It is no good feeling sorry for yourself. Did you call on Liz, as the rector suggested?'

He ignored this remark and headed for the kitchen.

'No, I thought not,' she said, following him. 'Well, go now. Tell her how you feel.' She perched herself on top of a tall, old fashioned fridge and dangled her feet over the side while Simon took two slices of bread from the bread bin and slapped them on the draining board. 'You'd better shift yourself, I want to get my lunch.'

She swung her legs round to the side while he plunged his head into the bowels of the fridge rooting out some rock hard butter, a small piece of cheddar and an overripe tomato, stationed between an onion and the remains of some overly green bacon.

'Liz doesn't want anything more to do with me,' he said, re-emerging.

'Why not?'

'You put the kibosh on everything that's why not. She thinks I'm nuts.'

'Nonsense.'

'Don't you nonsense me!' he stormed, waving the tomato in her face. 'Have you any idea what it's like having your life invaded by a ghost? Daft question – of course you haven't. You're pernicious you know that? You have destroyed my friendship with Liz, almost ruined my church career and there is now a question mark over my sanity.'

'How funny.'

'It is not funny,' he yelled. 'How dare you invade my life

and how dare you sit on my fridge. Get off!'

Adelina sighed and floated to the floor. 'You are behaving just as I did, when I thought I would never learn to glide. I blamed Thomas because he was never around when I needed him.'

'I fail to see what that has to do with anything.'

'You are frustrated.'

'Well, I know that.'

'You must take responsibility for your actions, instead of blaming the first thing to hand which just happens to be me.'

'You're a mischief maker of the worst kind,' he seethed, slicing his sandwich savagely in two. Tomato oozed from the sides, squirting his face and spraying a fine jet of pips over his shirt. He threw down his knife in rage. 'I can't stand any more.'

'Simon?'

'What?'

'I came to say that I am sorry. I want to make amends.'

'It's a bit late for that now.' He reached for the dishcloth and dabbed furiously at his shirt.

'It need not be too late. Go and see Liz.'

'What for? She'll only show me the door.'

'You assume she is leaving Chinkton Green on your account. That is arrogant of you, Simon. She may have an ailing mother in Ealing, or wish to spend her money on foreign travel. Whatever the reason unless you talk to her, you may never learn the truth.'

He threw the cloth at the sink. 'What are you? Some kind of dysfunctional fairy godmother?'

'If you visit Liz, you will help her to make up her mind.'

Adelina glided out of the kitchen into the hall and through the closed front door. 'Goodbye Simon,' she said, turning to face him.

'You're going?' Had he heard right?

'Yes.'

'Forever?'

'Yes. I will not trouble you again.'

She glided up the garden path.

'Well, all the best then,' he said. 'Hope your husband settles in all right.'

'Thank you. Give Pushka my love. I shall miss her.'

'I most certainly will.' Suddenly embarrassed, he bent to pluck a clump of bind-weed out of his flower-bed. When he stood up, she had gone.

Why did he feel so flat? he wondered, returning to the kitchen. His appetite had gone, and throwing his sandwich into the bin, he switched on the radio for company. In a minute he would go out and buy a newspaper – do a spot of visiting. That would take his mind off things.

'Hello Simon.'

He swung round. 'Liz!'

'The front door was open. Hope you don't mind.'

Mind? He was elated.

'Pushka's gone missing again, Simon. You seem to have a way with cats. Is she with you by any chance?'

'Pushka? No. No, not this time. I can categorically say with the utmost truth that I have not seen her.'

She turned to go. 'Oh well, thought it was worth a try.'

'How are you Liz?'

'Fine. Very busy, you know.'

'Of course.'

'And you?'

'Fine. Very busy too. Plenty to do in a parish.'

'Yes.' She hesitated. 'I'd better be getting back. Gerald will be chomping at the bit. You know how he is.'

'Absolutely! Terrifying!'

She smiled. 'Well bye, Simon.'

'Bye Liz.'

He saw her to the front door, watched her walk down the path, disappear up the lane away from his life forever. Oh, well, she probably wasn't his type anyway – too sophisticated, too worldly. He supposed he would end up with some mousy woman, large about the hips, who worked for the council and was good at accounts. Pratt! He should have offered her a cup of tea – why hadn't he? It would have at least given him another chance to explain things.

Simon sank into an armchair. What was the use? She didn't want to know. In any case what could he say? His story would sound wackier by the minute. OK. Do something physical, clean the fridge, clear the head. Why couldn't Gerald look for his own blasted cat? Why should a busy woman like Liz, have to run around after him? He stopped. Was it possible that she had volunteered to check Pushka's whereabouts?

'You just might have a point, Adelina,' he muttered, grabbing his coat from the stairs and making for the front door. He would clean the fridge later.

seventeen

'Hello Simon.'

'Liz I …'

'It's all right. You don't have to explain. Come in.'

'But I do. I want to say again how sorry I am for the way I behaved at the theatre.'

'If only you'd said.'

He followed her into the sitting room. 'Said what?'

'If you'd only told me. Poor you, I'd no idea.'

'No idea?'

'It can't be easy – coping with a psychotic relative.'

Simon stared. 'Who eh, told you about my aunt?'

'Mrs Herbert from the post office; and the church warden told her.'

'I see.' For once Charles Neville had done him a service. 'No doubt you heard about the missing urn as well?'

'Yes, I did. Your aunt again?'

Oh what wide, lucent eyes! How he loved her.

'No wonder you were acting so strangely at the theatre, Simon, with your aunt running a muck and everything. What are you going to do about her?'

'Do about her? Why, nothing.'

'You can't do nothing!'

'She'll just have to learn to cope.' Couldn't they leave the subject? He didn't want to argue.

'But she needs help, poor woman.' He watched Liz lace her brow with the finest of lines. 'Has she seen a psychiatrist?'

'It's being arranged,' he said hurriedly. 'Mm! Is that coffee I smell?'

'No,' she smiled. 'But I can make some, if you like.'

'That would be nice.' He followed her into the kitchen. 'Not in London today then?'

'I'm working from home this week.' She filled the kettle; laid a tray.

'Ah, very sensible,' he said. 'Nothing like the countryside to help you think – clears the head.'

'I suppose so.'

He watched her spoon coffee into two mugs. 'Liz?'

'Yes?'

'Is it true that you're thinking of leaving the village?'

She laughed now. 'News travels fast here, doesn't it? I've been thinking about it, yes.'

There was a knock on the door and then, 'Anyone home?'

Simon jumped. 'Who's that?'

'It's only next door.' Liz dropped the packet of biscuits she was holding and shot out of the kitchen.

'I'm just off, sweetie,' breezed Gerald, barely acknowledging Simon who had followed her into the sitting room.

Liz said, 'You look very smart, Gerald.'

'Do you like it? You never know what to wear for these castings. The agent said smart casual so I bought this new blazer. Do you think it's all right? Not too blue?'

'It's fine. Very becoming. Anyway, all the best, Gerald.'

'Oh, darling, don't!' He placed an elegantly, ringed hand on his chest while checking his appearance in the mirror. 'It's for the new coffee ad. I doubt I'll get it, but you have to show willing, don't you? Now flicking a stray hair out of his eye, 'I've left Pushka's evening meal on the side, over by my welsh dresser. Feed her when she wakes. She's sleeping like a babe at the minute – has been on and off all morning. Hope she's not sickening for something. Anyway, if you could just pop in every half hour.' He wrinkled his nose – a gesture of affection, Simon supposed.

'What time will you be back?'

'Who knows? You can be in and out at these castings, or be there forever. But hopefully not late. You've got the spare key?'

Liz nodded.

'Must rush then. Thanks a million.' He hesitated. 'Now you'll be all right with her?'

'Yes, yes. Don't worry.'

'Guard her with your life, sweetie.' And blowing a kiss, he shot off, leaving in his wake, a heady smell of French after-shave.

'What was all that about?' asked Simon.

'Can't you guess?' She began plumping up the sofa cushions.

'You're looking after Pushka? That bit's obvious,' he said, sitting on the sofa and watching Liz bite her lip – not look at him. 'He found the cat, I take it.'

She avoided the question – spoke airily. 'I'm looking after her while he goes up to London for this audition – a casting for some television commercial or something.'

'Yes, he said. So why did you come over to my place?'

'Oh, Simon!' Liz collapsed beside him. 'Do I have to spell it out? It was a ruse, silly. I had to think of some excuse – wanted to see you again, patch up our quarrel, say I'm sorry, do this …' She leaned over, cupped his face in her hands and kissed him hard on the mouth. 'There! I feel better now.' And picking up a cushion, tossed it playfully at his chest.

Simon's smile stretched from ear to ear as he laid the cushion aside and took her in his arms. '*The clouds ye so much dread are big with mercy, and shall break in blessings on your head,*' he murmured, nibbling her left ear.

'What was that?'

'Cowper. Words by the poet, William Cowper.'

'You smell of tomatoes,' she said, and kissed him again.

∅ ∅

Freddie was polishing the silver. He liked this job; it gave him time to reflect, daydream and plan. And it was a pleasure and a privilege to be entrusted with cleaning the many precious pieces that belonged to Sir Lionel and Lady Wilham, especially the eighteenth century French tea service with its fruit and flower cartouches. He enjoyed holding the dainty manicure sets and snuffboxes. It was like touching a bit of history. Freddie made up his mind to study antiques properly one day, maybe have a stall at an antique fair. He and Sophie could run that as a sideline. Yeah, that would be good.

It all seemed like a dream now, he thought, as he polished a gilt cast silver-serving spoon. There was nothing like a bit of polishing to bring you back to normal. He smiled as he remembered Sophie sitting up in their bed at The Black Dog Inn, waiting to tell him the news.

'Egbert's gone,' she had said.

'How do you know?'

'Adelina came to see me.'

'Came to see you? Here – in this room?'

'Yes. She told me that she could glide now. She taught herself in the end. So she zoomed up here to tell me and then zoomed back to the manor again with no problem. Great, isn't it? But the best news is that Egbert went back to the manor on his own – under his steam, or I should say, his own light. He didn't need us in the end, after all.'

Freddie flopped face down onto the bed. 'Wouldn't you know it? We come all the way to Windermere, brazen things out with old Doris, nearly get eaten by a pig and then Egbert calmly floats off under his own steam.'

'Don't be like that.' She stroked his hair.

'So let me get this straight,' he said, rolling onto his back. 'Adelina can glide, Egbert has been released and we can go home.'

'You don't sound very pleased,' she teased, kissing the top of his head.

'I am, of course I am. But I've had one hell of a night with Doris bawling her eyes out. I had to man the bar she was in such a state, and of course, there was no Harold to help out. Doris was plastered by the time I helped her up to bed.'

'She was really that drunk?'

Freddie nodded. 'Every time a customer asked her where Harold was, the tears started, so then she would disappear into the office for a "medicinal" brandy, as she termed it. It's incredible isn't it? She treated her husband like dirt when he was around but now that he's gone, she's praising him like he's the pope, or someone.' He pulled her down on top of him. 'Back to Chinkton Green tomorrow then.'

'Adelina sends her love and says, thank you.'

'Does she now?' he murmured, gently lifting her nightie over her head before burying his face in her breasts.

'She does. What's more, she wants to give us a present.'

'Really?' Running his hand down her side and tracing his finger around a small mole on her thigh. 'I wonder what it will be.'

Best not get steamed up, thought Freddie, laying aside the newly polished spoon before giving a final buff to a Regency dish with a moulded border.

'Penny for 'em,' said one of the housemaids coming into the scullery.

'Not fit for your tender ears, Daise. How are you doing?'

'Not as I can complain. Silver's looking nice.'

'Thanks.'

'Her ladyship wants to see you in the drawing room.' She opened the back door and gave her duster a sharp shake. 'Cor, it's nippy out. Soon be Christmas and a white one, I wouldn't wonder.'

'Don't wish your life away, Daise. We've another few weeks yet,' he said, removing his green apron and donning a black jacket.

Reaching the drawing room, he paused before giving his customary knock. Freddie always felt nervous when summoned by Lady Wilham. She could be quite formidable sometimes. He supposed that was the right and proper way to treat staff, distant like. You kept their respect that way. He had thought about his job quite a bit lately and wasn't sure she'd done him a favour giving him the grand title of butler. He didn't think he merited it one bit. What had he done? Fetched up a few bottles of wine from the cellar? Answered the door? Freddie had looked up the meaning of the word, in his old school dictionary: a male servant who looked after the table, wine and the general supervision of the staff. Well, he hadn't done any of that – not much of it anyway. There hadn't been a single dinner party since he'd come and the staff, such as they were, ran themselves and if anything, told him what to do. It had been okay at first, but quite a lot of water had gone under the bridge since he had started, well, a lot of water, and he wanted more now, wanted to make something of himself, especially since he and Sophie had become an item. It was important to think of their future together and just being Mr Fixit around the manor was not the way he intended spending the rest of his life.

'Come in.' Lady Wilham was standing by the fireplace holding a letter. Her face was flushed. 'Freddie. I've had some news – good news. Sir Lionel is returning to the manor sooner than expected. Next Monday, actually.'

'That is good news, madam.'

'Yes.' She paused. 'Do you enjoy working for us here,

Freddie?'

'Yes, madam.' He would like to have said more but something told him to keep quiet.

'I'm glad to hear it. I'm pleased with you, Freddie. You are thorough and trustworthy and have shown yourself efficient in a crisis.'

'Thank you madam.'

'You know, it hasn't been easy for any of us – the disturbances.' She broke off. 'But hopefully that's all in the past now.'

'I hope so, madam.'

'It was sad to lose our resident ghost, of course.' Then hurriedly adding, 'Not that I really believed in her, you understand. We, Sir Lionel and I, think it is important to employ a small nucleus of reliable, conscientious people. You, Freddie,' studying him thoughtfully, 'I feel that you can be trusted.'

'Thank you madam.'

She paused. 'All is quite peaceful here now, don't you think?'

'Oh, definitely, madam.'

'No more disturbances?'

'None.'

She walked to the window, turned and faced him. 'I don't think that I've been entirely fair with you, Freddie.'

Here we go; she's going to give me the chop, he thought, as he stared ahead, bracing himself for the worst. Out of the corner of his eye he saw something move. He stifled a cry. There in the corner, swinging to and fro on the rocking chair sat Adelina.

'Is something wrong, Freddie?' Lady Wilham asked sharply. 'You appear distracted.'

'Wrong?' Freddie swallowed. 'Nothing is wrong madam.'

'Why were you looking at that rocking chair?'

'I was just admiring its line. No other reason.'

'You are sure about that?'

'Quite sure.'

'Very well.' A sigh. 'Now, what was I saying?'

'You were saying something about fairness.'

'Ah, yes. Sir Lionel is a very hard working man, you know. He is a great conservationist but he also loves entertaining.' She smiled. 'I realise there hasn't been much of that since he went away, and your role of butler has, in a sense, been in name only – hardly fulfilling, I'd say.' Her eyes twinkled. 'So I have a suggestion to make. I would like you to go away for professional training.'

'Training?'

'Yes. To become a butler: a fully qualified butler. Does the idea appeal to you?'

He beamed. 'It appeals very much, madam.'

'There is a good training school in London where they can direct you in all areas of the job. It goes without saying that expenses will be paid, including your living costs. In your absence I shall employ temporary staff to manage your existing duties.'

'Yes, madam.'

'Naturally I need to send away for the prospectus and then we will take it from there, discuss the details and so on. In the meantime, if you would continue as usual that would be most satisfactory.'

'It will be a pleasure and thank you. I really appreciate your doing this for me.'

'I think,' she said, smiling broadly, 'that you will make an excellent butler.'

On his way out, he glanced again at the rocking chair. It was still swaying but Adelina had gone. Maybe this sudden promotion was her doing: a gift to him and Sophie – her way of saying thank you to them both.

Returning to the scullery, he sat at the table and admired his morning's work. He thought with pleasure of the wines that he would soon be serving, of the doors he would be opening and the staff that he would be supervising. Freddie glanced at his watch. It was four thirty. Another hour to go before Sophie got home from work. He smiled, a broad happy smile. He could wait – he would wait and phone her then and surprise her with the news.

Jane Lockyer Willis

Jane grew up in Warwickshire before moving to London to study English, Speech and Drama at The Guildhall School of Music and Drama:

Past experience includes the stage, amateur and professional; acting in plays for BBC World Service Radio and teaching. For many years she ran her own company, Speakwell Communications, offering tuition to adults in modulation, pronunciation, and presentation skills.

Jane has written a number of stage and audio plays, some of which have been performed here and abroad and she is a member of *The Society of Women Writers & Journalists.*

Her short stories have won The Irene Swarbrick Award, the John Walter Award twice, and for poetry, The Elizabeth Longford Award. ***Guys and Ghosts*** is her first full length novel.

Also by Jane & TSL: ***Tea at the Opalaco and other short stories***

Please visit Jane's website:
(http://playsbyjanelockyerwillis.co.uk/) or
Facebook page (PLAYS BY JANE LOCKYER WILLIS)
to see more on her plays.

www.ingramcontent.com/pod-product-compliance
Lightning Source LLC
Chambersburg PA
CBHW051140020726
47501CB00005B/1598